Miracle

ON **49**th STREET

Miracle

ON 49th STREET

MIKE
LUPICA

PHILOMEL BOOKS

PHILOMEL BOOKS A division of Penguin Young Readers Group. Published by The Penguin Group. Penguin Group (USA) Inc., 375 Hudson Street, New York, NY 10014, U.S.A. Penguin Group (Canada), 90 Eglinton Avenue East, Suite 700, Toronto, Ontario, Canada M4P 2Y3 (a division of Pearson Penguin Canada Inc.) Penguin Books Ltd, 80 Strand, London WC2R 0RL, England. Penguin Ireland, 25 St. Stephen's Green, Dublin 2, Ireland (a division of Penguin Books Ltd.) Penguin Group (Australia), 250 Camberwell Road, Camberwell, Victoria 3124, Australia (a division of Pearson Australia Group Pty Ltd). Penguin Books India Pvt Ltd, 11 Community Centre, Panchsheel Park, New Delhi—110 017, India. Penguin Group (NZ), Cnr Airborne and Rosedale Roads, Albany, Auckland 1310, New Zealand (a division of Pearson New Zealand Ltd). Penguin Books (South Africa) (Pty) Ltd, 24 Sturdee Avenue, Rosebank, Johannesburg 2196, South Africa. Penguin Books Ltd, Registered Offices: 80 Strand, London WC2R 0RL, England.

Design by Gina DiMassi. Text set in Wilke Roman. Library of Congress Cataloging-in-Publication Data Lupica, Mike. Miracle on 49th Street / Mike Lupica. p. cm. Summary: After her mother's death, twelve-year-old Molly learns that her father is a basketball star for the Boston Celtics. [1. Fathers and daughters—Fiction. 2. Interpersonal relations—Fiction. 3. Basketball—Fiction. 4. Boston (Mass.)—Fiction.] I. Title: Miracle on Forty-ninth Street. II. Title: Miracle on 49th St. III. Title: Miracle on Forty-ninth St. IV. Title. PZ7.L97914Mir 2006 [Fic]—dc22 2005032648 ISBN 0-399-24488-3

1 3 5 7 9 10 8 6 4 2

First Impression

These books are family efforts,
which is why they are always dedicated to my wife,
and my three sons, and my daughter.
But I really needed my daughter on this one,
because this one is about a twelve-year-old girl
who is beautiful and brave and funny and smart.

So I just imagined what Hannah Grace
would be like at twelve.

ACKNOWLEDGMENTS

William Goldman, Susan Burden, Esther Newberg:
They are in on it from the start, and never too busy to read.

And Michael Green:
Who got me to scribble at his desk
one day before lunch. That's where both of us
first met Miss Molly Parker.

CHAPTER 1

*M*olly Parker wasn't here for some stupid autograph.

She wasn't even here for the open practice the Celtics had run today, their last practice before they would begin the regular season tomorrow night against the 76ers. Though she had to admit that it was pretty cool to sit with the other kids and their parents inside the Celtics' practice gym at the Sports Authority Training Center at HealthPoint, which didn't so much sound like the name of a basketball court but the answer to some kind of essay question.

The Celtics had scheduled their annual Kids Day practice at four o'clock so that the parents—moms mostly, Molly noticed that right off—could pick up their kids at school or at the bus and get them here on time. Molly, who'd gotten out here to Waltham early, had watched a lot of them pull up to the entrance to the big public parking lot on the side, feeling as if she were watching some kind of parade for SUVs.

Yuppie limos, her mom liked to call them.

Of course, then her mom would wonder if anybody in America even used the word *yuppie* anymore, or if there was

1

some kind of new description for all the moms driving Suburbans and Land Cruisers and Explorers.

"Pretty soon there'll be double-decker versions of these monsters," Jennifer Parker would say to Molly. "Like our red London buses."

When they had finally come back for good from London, the only place Molly had ever thought of as home, her mom had acted as if everything was new to her, as if the country she'd grown up in had now become foreign, just because she'd been away for over twelve years.

One day when they were driving on the Mass Pike, Jennifer Parker—Jen to her friends—had found herself in the middle lane, with big SUVs on both sides of their rented Taurus.

"Okay," her mom said, "that's it. I know we've only been back a few weeks, but they're going to need to build a bigger country."

"Mom," Molly said that day, "you're going to have to let go on the whole car thing."

Her mom grinned then, because she was the coolest and always got the joke.

"Did I ever by any chance mention the Volkswagen bug I used to drive around in college?"

And Molly had said, "Oh, no, Mom. Never. Not one single time. No kidding—you used to have a Volkswagen bug in college? It wasn't fire-engine red by any chance, was it?"

Then they'd both laughed. Because they both always got the joke, even if it was one as old as the one about her old college car.

In the players' parking lot now, behind the Sports Authority building, leaning against the wheel of *his* SUV, Molly closed her eyes, picturing her and her mother in the front seat of the rented car that day, waiting to see how that particular snapshot, from the album she carried around her head, was going to affect her.

Nothing today.

Progress, Molly thought.

Or maybe progress had not one stinking thing to do with it, maybe she was just too wired—a Mom word—to focus on anything except what was going to happen next.

Practice had been over for twenty minutes or so. The players had scattered to different points on the court to sign autographs. All the players except the one the kids in the house really wanted: Josh Cameron.

Not just the biggest star on the Celtics, but the biggest star in the NBA, and maybe any sport right now.

One of the young guys who worked for the Celtics had gotten on the microphone and said that because they knew it would be a mob scene if Josh tried to sign something for every boy and girl in the gym, he—Josh—had a surprise for them all. In the lobby waiting for them on the way out, the guy from the Celtics said, everyone in attendance today would be handed a special Josh Cameron goody bag. Inside was an autographed youth basketball, Celtics cap, and a T-shirt from Josh's summer basketball camp in Maine.

Then Josh Cameron himself, looking a little bigger to Molly than he did on television, maybe because he wasn't standing next to some seven-foot monster type, took the microphone and personally thanked everybody for coming, said he hoped they'd had a great time, and promised them a great Celtics season.

"Always remember," he said, "we can't do it without your support. And I mean you guys."

"You're my hero, Josh!" a girl yelled from somewhere in the stands.

He smiled and wagged a finger in her direction, like she'd somehow shouted out the wrong answer.

"No," he said. "You guys are *my* heroes."

He told them to enjoy their goody bags, told them to study real hard when they weren't rooting their hardest for the Celtics, then left the practice gym.

That was Molly's cue to beat it out of there, sneaking through a side door she'd scoped out as the other kids were making their way down to the court. She didn't even bother to go to the lobby and pick up the bag with all the cute stuff inside.

Instead she went straight for where she'd seen Josh Cameron's black Lincoln Navigator parked. Molly didn't know anything about cars, not really. But she knew what Josh was driving because he'd won it for being MVP of the NBA Finals five months ago.

Molly knew about the black Lincoln Navigator the way she knew everything there was to know about him by now. Sometimes her buddy Sam would quiz her, out of the blue, no matter what they were doing.

"What kind of watch does he wear?"

"Too easy," she'd say. "Omega. They use him now instead of the guy who used to play James Bond."

"Deodorant?"

"Red Zone from Old Spice. C'mon, these aren't even challenging."

"Okay, how about this? What's the name of his new Labrador puppy, the one he just got last week?"

"He got a new puppy last week?"

Sam made a sound like a buzzer going off on one of the game shows he made Molly watch sometimes on the Game Show Network.

"Nah," Sam said. "I made it up. But I had you going for a minute. You thought I knew something about him that you didn't."

"But you didn't. Know something I didn't, I mean."

"But I did. Have you going. Which is enough to make my day, frankly."

"You're crazy," Molly said.

"What does that say about you?" Sam said. "You could have picked anybody to be your friend and picked me."

"Good point," she said.

If Molly didn't know everything important there was to know about Josh Cameron, she was sure she knew more than anybody else. Her mom had called it the joy of Google.

"I'm not big on technology," her mom would say, and then Molly would slap her forehead and say, "You have got to be kidding, Mom! I never heard that one before, either."

"But," her mom would say, ignoring her, "I do feel that life got a lot better when *Google* became a verb."

By now Molly Parker had Googled Josh Cameron so many times that she knew his first two Google pages, starting with his own Web site, by heart.

Basically, he was the most famous and best Boston Celtics

basketball player since Larry Bird. And the best and flashiest point guard they'd had since Bob Cousy. But most people, Molly had found out in her research, seemed to think Josh Cameron was the basketball equivalent of Tom Brady, the Patriots quarterback who won all the Super Bowls and looked like he should be playing Hilary Duff's boyfriend in the movies, even if he was waaaaay too old for her.

Basically, Josh Cameron, six feet two, out of the University of Connecticut, winner of four NBA titles in his first nine years in the league, was the biggest and most popular star in sports right now. American sports, anyway. Molly didn't even try to explain to Sam or any of the other kids she went to school with about the whole David Beckham thing.

He was thirty-one now, about the same age as her mom. It wasn't Cryptkeeper old, but he was getting up there, even if you couldn't tell it by the way he was playing. The Celtics had just won again, and he had won another MVP award.

"He's one of those guys," Jen Parker told her daughter. "He'll get old about the same time Peter Pan does."

Now, after the T rides she had taken to get to the buses and then the walk from the last bus station, which seemed like a lot more than the mile the bus driver had said, she was finally going to meet him.

She had decided it was time.

She knew it would make everybody mad that she had skipped out of school early again with a made-up story, at least when they figured out she hadn't gone to Sam's house after school like she'd said. Molly didn't care. She knew they'd try to act all worried about her when she got home, but it would just mean that she'd inconvenienced everybody.

Again.

Molly the Inconvenience.

She took out her cell phone as a way of reminding herself to turn it off when she saw him coming. She knew that any kid her age with her own cell phone was supposed to consider that a huge deal. Not Molly. The Nokia she carried in the front pocket of her jeans always seemed to her like the business end of some long leash, one that stretched all the way to the Sports Authority Training Center from the old brownstone in the part of Boston known as Beacon Hill.

She tried to look through the smoked windows of the Navigator, wanting to see if it was true that he really had a portable fax machine in there. Molly knew about that the way she knew that Cherry Garcia ice cream was his favorite and that he had every single Rolling Stones song ever on his iPod and that . . .

She didn't just *know*.

She *really* knew.

It was why Sam was always making fun of her, even though he always had a sense when to back off, because in the end this was what they both knew:

This wasn't funny.

She decided to check the phone for messages real fast, just to see if they'd called Sam's house yet looking for her. Checking up on her.

One text message.

From Sam.

Pretty much her only real friend.

HOWS IT GOIN MOLS?

Molly was no big fan of text messaging. It made her feel as if she was five years old all over again and trying to spell out words by picking them out of her alphabet soup.

But she knew that if she didn't answer Sam, he'd just keep messaging her until she did.

ANYTIMENOW. STA TUNED.

Molly saw Josh Cameron now.

Saw him come out the door you could barely tell was a door. It was like a piece of the brick wall that just opened by magic, underneath one of the giant glass windows.

Molly's head poked just over the hood of the car.

He was alone, the way she'd hoped he would be, wearing jeans with holes in the knees and untied high-top sneaks and carrying a green Celtics bag. And he was wearing the leather jacket she somehow knew he'd be wearing, his favorite single item of clothing going all the way back to the University of Connecticut. And the wraparound sunglasses she knew were Oakleys, because they were the exact same glasses he wore in a new television commercial.

Molly had read a story about him in which one of his teammates, Nick Tutts, had said that his buddy Josh Cameron went through life as he if he owned the place. The writer had asked, "What place?" And Nick Tutts said, "*Any*place."

That was how Josh looked to Molly now as he moved across the parking lot, fifty yards away, then twenty, pointing with his car keys now and unlocking the doors to the Navigator. Not just unlocking it, but turning the engine on at the same time!

She found herself thinking how awesome Sam would think that was, Sam being a gadget guy.

That was for later. For now, she took a deep breath and stepped out from behind the car.

"Hey," she said.

He smiled. But it was one of those smiles like he was smiling right through her or past her.

Shaking his head at the same time.

"Sorry," he said. "No autographs. It wouldn't be fair to the others."

Molly said, "Don't want one."

Josh said, "You know, you really shouldn't be in the parking lot. Everybody was sort of supposed to stay in the gym when practice was over."

"I snuck out early," Molly said. "I needed to talk to you."

Be cool, fool, Sam had said. Don't get ahead of yourself.

Josh Cameron looked back over his shoulder, toward the gate, as if maybe the guard could help him out here.

"Listen, honey, I don't mean to blow you off."

"Molly," she said. "My name's Molly."

"Molly," he said. "Nice to meet you, Molly. But, listen, I'm run-

9

ning kind of late. We've got our Welcome Home dinner later, in town, and I've got to get ready for it."

"At the Westin," Molly said.

"Right. So I need to get back and change and do a few things."

He took the Oakleys off now, as if giving her a closer look. "Do I know you?"

Molly was the one shaking her head now. "No reason why you should." Then, "Nice jacket."

"This old thing? We go way back, the two of us."

"To UConn. I know."

"Yeah, the sportswriters seem to get a kick out of it, maybe because they always think this is the year when it's finally going to fall apart." He shrugged. "No kidding, I don't want to be rude, but I gotta bounce."

He opened the door on the driver's side, like this was the official beginning of him saying good-bye to her and driving away.

Blowing her off.

He tossed the Celtics bag on the passenger seat in the front, then said, "Hey!" Like he'd come up with a bright idea. "Hey, I've got something for you, after all." Winking at her. "Even though I said no autographs."

He opened up the back door then, pulled out a regulation size basketball, grabbed a Sharpie out of one of the pockets of the leather jacket. "To Molly—is that okay?"—not even waiting for an answer as he started writing.

When he was done, he handed her the ball. She looked at what he'd written. "To Molly, a great fan and a new friend. Josh Cameron, No. 3."

Molly turned the ball over in her hands.

Then she handed it back.

It actually got a laugh out of him. "Now, wait a second. Nobody *ever* passes up Josh Cameron stuff." He put his hands to his cheeks, trying to make himself look sad. "I must be losing it."

Get to it, she told herself, you're losing him.

"I didn't come here for stuff," she said.

"Why did you then?"

Here goes.

"I needed to talk to you about something important."

He looked at his Omega James Bond watch.

"You know what's important to me right now? Making sure I show up for that Welcome Home dinner on time. So how about you have your teacher or your parents call the PR department and, who knows, maybe I could come speak at your school sometime."

Then he slid in behind the wheel and reached for the door and said, "Nice meeting you, Molly."

"She bought that jacket for you."

He turned off the ignition now and said, "Excuse me?"

"She said she had left you crying in your dorm room when you got back that night from not making the Final Four, saying it was all your fault and you had let everybody down. And the next day she went and spent all the money she had in her checking account on that jacket and told you the next year you could wear it to the Final Four. And you did."

She said it word for word exactly right, the way she had all the times when she'd rehearsed it with Sam, Sam playing the part of Josh Cameron.

He got out of the car and closed the door and got down in a crouch, so they were eye to eye. "You're Jen's kid, aren't you?"

"Yes," she said.

"I've always told people that this old jacket is my good luck charm," he said. "But I never told why. We promised we'd never tell anybody."

"Don't be mad," Molly said. "She only told me."

"I'm not mad."

"She told me she never broke promises. Even when she promised you she wasn't ever coming back."

Molly was wearing a red cap Sam had given her, a Red Sox cap with "Believe" on the front, from the year they won the World Series. Josh tipped it back slightly, to give himself a better look at her. "No wonder I thought I might know you," he said. Then he nodded and said, "So she finally did come back."

Molly tried to swallow but couldn't. "She came back."

"Well, tell your mom she didn't have to send you if she wanted to let me know she was back. She could've come herself."

Molly said, "No."

"Same old stubborn Jen. And she used to say I was the one who'd never change."

"My mom died," Molly said. "Right before school started."

She watched as Josh Cameron started to fall backward, before he caught himself at the last second. "No," he said. "Oh, God, no."

Then he said, "How?"

"It was cancer," Molly said. "They found out about it too late, that's what the doctors back in London told her. Then she came home, and the doctors here told her the exact same thing."

He took her hands. "I am so sorry, kid. Thank you for coming out here to tell me, or I never would've known. I mean, I didn't even know she got married over there."

Molly said, "She didn't, actually."

"Oh," he said. He ran a hand through his hair, like he was stumped, and finally said, "Well, okay then."

"It's cool," she said.

"Well, at least I understand why you didn't want some silly old signed ball. What you had to tell me *was* important."

"That wasn't it," Molly said. "At least not all of it."

"I don't understand."

Molly couldn't help it, she found herself smiling now, hearing her mom's voice inside her head like she was right there with them.

Which maybe she was.

The idea that she was being one of the things that kept Molly going.

"Mom said there was a lot you didn't understand."

"Yeah," he said. "She did."

He looked past Molly, like he was looking to some faraway place in the distance, and said, "She used to say that a lot, as a matter of fact."

"See, I wasn't supposed to come . . . she kept saying it was a truly bad idea . . ." The words were spilling out of her now. "And if you know my mom—what am I saying? You *did* know her . . . you know what it was like when she said something was truly good or truly bad . . ."

"Molly," he said, "*what* was this truly bad idea?"

"Me telling you that you're my dad."

$\mathcal{J}$n the distance, Molly noticed some of the other Celtics players coming out of the Sports Authority Training Center.

"No," Josh Cameron finally said to her.

He straightened up now, grunting a little as he did, as if doing that made his knees hurt.

"Excuse me?" she said, acting as if she hadn't heard him correctly, even though it was just one word in the air between them.

No.

"I don't believe you," he said.

"It's true!" Molly said, louder than she meant. "You have to believe me."

As soon as she heard the last part come out of her mouth, she knew she sounded as if she were six years old instead of twelve.

She put her hand on the back pocket of her jeans, where she had the letter her mom had written to her, one of the letters she had left for Molly to read after she was gone. Jen Parker, who had really wanted to be a writer. Who said that she was always better at writing her thoughts down than saying them out loud.

Molly had planned on showing him the letter, but now she wondered what the point was.

This wasn't going anything like she'd planned.

"Keep your voice down," Josh said, looking past her to where some of his teammates, one of them the big Chinese rookie, Ming Cho, were getting into their own Navigator-type cars.

"I'm sorry," Molly said.

Then thought to herself, *You're* sorry? You tell him what you just told him and he basically calls you a liar and then tells you to shut up, like he's a teacher in class, and *you're* the one who's supposed to apologize?

Who are you, Barbie?

Forget sounding six. She sounded like the girly girl of the universe.

"Listen," he said. "I'm sorry I snapped at you. I am sorry about your mom, because she must have told you I cared about her a lot once. And I'm sure that if you don't know who— If you don't have a dad, it must be even harder on you. But that doesn't mean you can just show up out of the blue and lay something like this on me."

He looked down.

The watch again.

Like they were nearing the end of the game.

Even if this was no game, at least not to her.

She said, "Why would I lie?"

"Only you can answer that one, kid." He tilted his head to the side, like he was curious about something. "Tell me again how old you are."

"I never told you how old I was. But I'm twelve."

Molly actually felt like she could see him doing the math, like his face was a blackboard and he was adding. Or subtracting.

"Junior year abroad," he said. "She had this figured pretty good."

"Had what figured pretty good?"

"The timing," Josh Cameron said. "To make her story plausible."

"Her *story*?" Molly could feel herself clenching her fists. "You think my mom made up this story and then told me to come tell it to you after she died?"

"It's a good try, is all I'm saying."

Molly took another deep breath, through her nose, then another, slowly, filling her lungs up, emptying them, one of the exercises the grief counselor had told her about.

She pictured herself throwing the letter at him, telling him if he wanted to really know her mom's *story*, well, here it was.

Only she didn't.

"It *was* junior year abroad," Molly said.

"When she left," he said. "Saying she didn't know when she'd be back."

Molly didn't say a word, still just trying to breathe in and out.

"Like I said," Josh said. "I'm sorry about all of this."

"You've made that pretty clear."

"But there is no way in this world that Jen . . . that your mom . . . could've gone off to London and had a baby—what you're trying to tell me now is my baby—and never told me about it over all these years."

Off to her left, Molly's eyes tracked on all the cars pulling away from the Sports Authority Training Center, the kids probably ripping through the goody bags in the backseats, the moms

16

driving them home with their stupid autographs and their Josh Cameron stuff.

Molly found herself thinking of Sam. Wishing she could text message him right this minute. Everybody else thought he was just some funny-looking nerd, but from the first day, Molly had been able to see inside him. She picked up right away that he was smarter than everybody else, that he was funnier, that he always knew the exact right thing to say.

Never once when they'd rehearsed her big scene had it played out like this.

Josh Cameron acting as if she'd just shown up here to throw up some kind of pathetic—*truly* pathetic—desperation shot at the buzzer.

"I don't even know where you live," he said. "Or who you live with. Do they know you came here today?"

Molly said, "I live with Mr. and Mrs. Evans. They have a daughter the same age as me. Mrs. Evans was my mom's best friend at UConn."

"You're living with Barbara?"

"On Joy Street. Near Beacon."

"Does Barbara think you're— Did your mom tell her the same story you're telling me?"

Her story. They were back to that.

The made-up kind of story is what he really meant.

"No," Molly said.

"It was between you and your mom."

"Pretty much. She said she'd made a promise to herself that she wasn't ever going to tell anybody."

"Until she was dying."

17

Molly said, "She wasn't even going to tell then. But she saw that the older I got, the more suspicious I was about what she'd always told me about my dad, that he was a soldier she'd met when she first got to London and then he went off and got himself killed in the first Gulf War."

"And you started to not believe her?"

"There was just a lot of things that didn't add up, is all."

"And when you finally got her to fess up, what was her reason for never telling you the truth—what she said was the truth—about me?"

Molly stared at him hard for a second and then said, "Because mom said you wouldn't have been any better at loving me than you were at loving her."

He slowly nodded his head. "Well, she still knows everything, doesn't she?" he said.

Then he opened the door to the Navigator, got behind the wheel, closed the door, started up the engine, and drove away.

CHAPTER 3

*S*he called Sam from the parking lot.

He asked how it had gone. She told him, finally saying that maybe things could have gone worse than they actually did, but only if Josh Cameron had told her she was grounded and taken away her computer privileges before he made his getaway.

Sam said, "He really thought you had made it up?"

"About my mom being my mom? No. About him being my dad? Yes."

"He's a freak."

Freak being one of Sam's favorite and most frequently used words. There were good freaks and bad freaks, depending on the situation. A mean teacher could be a freak. Bad. A rock star or a ballplayer or an actor on a TV show could be a freak. Good. Parents could go either way, depending on the situation.

"Get back here as soon as you can," Sam said. "Before my mom gets home from Paper and Scissors." It was the art class for little kids that Sam's mom taught a few days a week at the Boston Public Library on Boylston Street, a few blocks from where they lived.

Molly said, "Has anybody called?"

"No," Sam said, "we're still good."

"No Barbara, calling to see if I really went there after school?"

"It's insane," Sam said. "She actually trusts you."

"What happens if she does call?"

"I've got the ringer turned off on the phone and a message that says that my mom's at work and that Jill the hated housekeeper took us over to the Public Gardens for a game of catch."

Sam refused, under penalty of torture, to ever refer to the hated Jill as a babysitter. He had told his mom he was twelve now and didn't need a babysitter. So here was the compromise: Jill's two days of cleaning the apartment were the two days that Emma would work in the late afternoon. But, officially, Jill was there to clean and not to watch Sam because that's what housekeepers who were *not* babysitters did.

"Catch?" Molly said. "As in baseball-like catch? As in you and me? There's a better chance of me trying to teach you cricket."

"My feeling, as you know, is that if you're going to make something up, make it a whopper."

"Yeah, with cheese," Molly said. "We have never once played catch in the park. Trust me, I'd remember."

"True," he said. "But they don't know that. I kind of like having old Barbara think I'm a secret jock, even with this bod."

Sam Bloom was basically shaped like a frog, although Molly would never tell him that. Somehow he seemed to get wider as he went from top to bottom. But to Molly, he was a fairy-tale frog who turned into a prince every time he opened his mouth and either smartened her up or made her laugh.

20

"I'm on my way," Molly said.

"Hurry," Sam said.

Molly said, "Yeah, I'll tell my limo driver to step on it."

She had brought forty dollars of her secret money, just in case she missed one of the buses on the way home or took the wrong one and needed to call a cab. "If I don't mess up, I can be there in an hour."

"If you're not, I'll stall somehow."

"Sam Bloom?"

They both knew that when she went first name and last name on him, she was more serious than a trip to the dentist's.

"Yes?" he said, trying to sound innocent.

"One whopper a day is enough."

"Mols, if I am forced to tell another lie, all I can tell you is that it will fit the occasion."

"That's what I'm afraid of."

"Let me ask you something," he said.

Molly realized that just talking to him on her cell was making her feel a little better already. "Shoot," she said.

"Who's got your back more than me?"

"No one," Molly said.

The truth was, nobody besides Sam Bloom had her back at all.

The Evanses lived in an old brownstone on a narrow cobblestone street. The actual address was 1A Joy Street. Molly now found that funny, just not ha-ha funny. She had told Sam once that if she did find any real joy at 1A Joy Street that she wanted to figure out a way to send up a flare.

Sam's apartment, closer to Kenmore Square than it was to the Public Gardens, was about a twenty-minute walk away, down Beacon. His father worked for Bank of America and seemed to be traveling all the time. His mom kept busy by working two days a week at Paper and Scissors, and another two at an exercise place called Exhale near the Four Seasons Hotel. Sam said it was full of women trying to look like his mom.

Sam thought it was one of God's jokes that a woman as pretty and fit as Emma Bloom would have a "lump" like him for a kid.

"You're not a lump, and don't let me ever hear you say that again," Molly told him. "One of these days everybody's going to see how great you truly are the way I do."

Truly.

A Mom word.

Sam Bloom was alone way too much until Molly came to Boston and she and her mom took a two-bedroom sublet in the same building where the Blooms lived, thinking they could extend the lease but never even making it to the end of it. . . .

Sam was waiting for her in the lobby of his building when Molly finally got there about six-thirty. He said that as soon as Jill the hated housekeeper finished talking to someone else from the Planet Ditz on her cell phone, she'd walk the two of them to Molly's.

"Does Jill even know I haven't been with you all this time?" Molly said.

"Just because there are so many things Jill doesn't know, you mean?"

"I was too polite to put it that way."

"Jill barely knows I've been with me the last few hours," Sam said.

Jill came downstairs when they buzzed her, doing what she did every single time she had to walk Molly home—acting as if they'd interrupted her in the middle of brain surgery.

"Let's get this over with," Jill said. "I've got some calls to make."

"There's people you know you *haven't* talked to yet today?" Sam said.

She gave him a look like he was a fly she couldn't swat.

"Love the orange streaks in your hair," Molly said.

"What*ever*!"

That was pretty much it for conversation the rest of the way. Before Sam left Molly at the front door, he whispered, "I'll call you when I get home."

Molly whispered back, "I don't think a lot is going to happen between now and then."

"You never know," Sam said.

Molly walked inside 1A Joy Street. Or 1A Joyless Street, which is the way she really thought of it. Not because of the Evanses. They seemed happy enough there and did their best to make Molly happy.

It just wasn't happening.

Barbara Evans was in the front hall, portable phone in her hand, looking totally bored at whatever she was hearing on the other end, making a spinning motion with her free hand like she wanted the other person to wrap things up sometime before Christmas.

When Molly walked in, Barbara looked as if the cavalry had just shown up.

"Listen, dear," Barbara said into the phone, "Molly just showed up, so I've got to run. I'll call you about the book fair tomorrow." After she clicked off, she said to herself, "Unless I change all of my phone numbers first."

To Molly she said, "Have a good time at the park with Sam?"

"It's always a good day when I'm with Sam," she said.

"Now, you know I *love* Sam Bloom," Barbara said. "But I do wish you'd expand your range of friends."

Molly said, "Why?"

"As a way of expanding your range of interests," Barbara said, though she never really explained what those interests should be.

"I'm working on it," Molly said.

"And you know that without forcing the *sister* thing on you"—she made little bracket marks around the word *sister*, the way she always did—"I would love it if you and Kimmy would spend a little more time together away from school."

Kimberly Anne Evans. Bill and Barbara's twelve-year-old daughter. And only child in the house until Molly showed up.

Kimmy, Molly had to admit, had been pretty great about Molly rocking her world this way, even though deep down she had to have liked things a lot better the way they were when there was only one little girl at 1A Joyless Street.

"Kimmy and I are cool," Molly said.

"I'm just going to assume that's a good thing."

"It is."

"Now, about dinner," Barbara said.

24

It was a game they played almost every night, as if Molly was helping Barbara plan that evening's menu. She'd ask if such and such a dish was okay, and Molly would say fine.

"Pasta with broccoli all right, hon?"

"Fine."

"We've got some new chocolate low-fat ice cream that tastes just like the real stuff for dessert."

Barbara assumed that everybody in the world counted calories as ferociously as she did.

"Can't wait," Molly said and started up the stairs just as Kimmy Evans came bursting through the front door the way she always did, as though she was about to tell you there was fire coming from an upstairs window.

Molly was halfway up the stairs to her room when she heard Kimmy say the following to her back:

"Molly Parker, I can't *believe* you got to watch Josh Cameron practice without me!"

CHAPTER 4

*I*t had never occurred to Molly that somebody else from their school—it was called the Prescott School, but Molly thought of it as the Precious School—would be at Celtics practice.

Or that if they *were* at practice, any of them would notice Molly underneath her Red Sox cap.

Except.

Except Andrew Safir's mom had taken him after school.

He had spotted Molly somehow, way at the top of the bleachers on the other side of the court. He'd tried to find her when it was time to go on the court for autographs, but she was gone.

When he'd gotten home, he'd called Paul Reilly.

Whose sister Caroline immediately instant messaged Kimmy Evans and asked why Molly had gotten to go watch the Celtics practice and she hadn't.

Which is why Molly stood there now in the Evanses' front hallway, having been told to march down those stairs right now, young lady, and was totally and screamingly busted.

* * *

"You went to see *Josh Cameron*?" Barbara said. "On your own? Without asking? Why in the world would you do something like that?"

"I wanted to tell him about Mom," Molly said.

"You couldn't ask me to do it? This wasn't something you felt you even had to discuss with me?"

Molly said, "You knew him in college, too. I figured that if you thought it was important—telling him my mom had died—you would've done it already."

It wasn't much, but it was all Molly had.

Kimmy had already gone to her room by this point, whispering, "I am soooooo sorry," as she walked past Molly.

Just Barbara and Molly now, Barbara not even wanting to take the scene into the living room. She wanted to have it out right here and right now. Molly half expected cartoon smoke to start coming out of her ears any second.

"So there was no need, in your mind, for us to even talk about this." Barbara hugged herself, like that was going to keep her from exploding all over the front hall. She started pacing in front of Molly, talking to herself as much as she was talking to Molly. "Good God. Josh Cameron."

"You sound madder that it was him than you do that I went up there without telling," Molly said.

Barbara stopped. "What does that mean?"

"It means I'm not sure what I'm in more trouble about," Molly said.

"You're in trouble for all of it!" Barbara said, shouting now. "I'm angry about all of it."

27

Molly had never seen her this angry about anything.

"I'm sorry," Molly said. "If I had thought—"

"You didn't think, that's the problem," Barbara said. "Did you?"

"I just saw where it was Kids Day at the Celtics practice place, and I couldn't take the chance you wouldn't bring me."

"So now you make up the rules for yourself around here?"

"I thought you said you liked Josh Cameron when you were all in college?" Molly said.

"No, I don't recall as how I ever said that, exactly."

"You weren't all friends?"

"He was your mom's boyfriend," she said. "I was her best friend. Let's just say we all made that work until he—until your mom went away. I hate to even say this to you, but it's something you're going to understand a lot better when you're older."

"So you *didn't* like him," Molly asked.

"It wasn't that I didn't like him," Barbara said. "I just didn't think he was right for your mom." She shook her head now. "Why are we even talking about this? The issue isn't what I did or did not think of Mr. Josh Cameron. The issue is you, young lady."

It was Molly's experience that "young lady" was never, ever good.

"I'm just trying to understand."

Barbara said, "Understand this: You don't just follow the rules you like around here and then make up the rest on your own."

Molly put her head down, wanting to get off the merry-go-round now, just wanting this to be over. She had known Barbara would rock her world once Kimmy spilled the beans. She just never expected it to be like this.

"Do you have anything else to say for yourself?" Barbara said now.

Molly shook her head.

Barbara said, "You've passed on your message to Josh Cameron. You've had your little adventure. Let's just have that be the end of it, please."

Molly thinking: If it wasn't just the beginning.

But keeping her mouth good and shut.

"How did you get there, if you don't mind me asking?"

"Trains and buses," Molly said. "If you can get around London on the tube, you can get to Waltham, believe me."

"You know I'm going to have to tell Bill about this when he gets home."

Her husband. He had a big job with a Tokyo bank based in Boston, and because of the huge time difference between Boston and Tokyo, it sometimes seemed to Molly as if he were working twenty-four hours a day. But he was nice to Molly when he was around, even if he didn't go out of his way, the way Barbara did, to make the whole situation at 1A Joyless seem completely wonderful and normal. Molly respected him for it, actually. He didn't try to play the part of her dad. He had told her that once, not long after her mom had died, stopping in her room before she went to bed.

"I can't be something I'm not," he'd said. "So I'm not going to even attempt to be the father you never had. The best I can hope for is to be your friend."

Molly said that was fine with her. It was the closest thing to a heart-to-heart talk they'd ever had. Ever since then, Molly always sort of thought that she and Bill Evans were pretty squared away on things.

She wasn't really his daughter.

She wasn't Barbara's daughter.

She wasn't Kimmy's sister.

That was the deal. And being a real family wasn't ever going to *be* the deal, no matter how hard Barbara tried.

"The two of us will decide what an appropriate response to this should be," Barbara said. "It's not even this crazy . . . adventure. It's the lie, Molly. I just can't tolerate lying."

"I know," Molly said. "That's the part I'm sorriest about."

Almost over now.

She even started inching back toward the stairs.

Barbara walked across the hall and gave Molly a hug, then quickly pulled back. "You're a member of this family now," she said.

Now *there* was a whopper.

"I know," Molly said.

"You're here because your mom and I both wanted you here," Barbara said. "I promised her I would take care of you. But I can only do that if you let me."

Molly looked down at her Converse basketball high-tops, the same ones Josh Cameron wore, with the green Celtics trim on them.

"It won't happen again," she said.

Not exactly a whopper.

Maybe a chicken nugget.

CHAPTER 5

I am soooo sorry," Kimmy said again. "If I had thought about this for, like, as long as it takes to dry my *hair*, I would have been able to figure out that if I didn't know you were going, then my *mom* couldn't possibly know you were going."

"No biggie," Molly said. "I knew I might get found out when I got up there."

Kimmy had been waiting in Molly's room, in the middle of her bed, hugging one of Molly's pillows and looking as if she might cry.

"I'll clean your room for a week," Kimmy said. "Two weeks. You name it."

"It was an accident," Molly said.

"I'll talk to my dad when he gets here," Kimmy said. "Do my daddy's-little-girl number on him. Never fails. What do you say to that?"

What Molly Parker desperately wanted to say: If you leave my room right this minute, I'll call the whole thing even, no matter what kind of punishment I get from your father.

But there were no short visits from Kimmy. There were no

short conversations. Kimmy could talk, Molly was thinking now, the way Josh Cameron could play basketball. She wasn't a clone of her mother. Kimmy actually looked more like her father and had his blue eyes and his long legs, but she had definitely inherited her mother's need for drama.

After all her years living in London, it sometimes made Molly think of the royal family.

She was living with the royal family of drama today. Queen Barbara and Princess Kimmy.

Molly said, "It's all right. Really."

"I waited my whole life to have somebody I could feel was like a sister," Kimmy said. "And now I pull something like this because of my big stupid mouth."

"You didn't mean to, that's what I keep trying to tell you."

Kimmy, she couldn't help but notice, was showing absolutely no signs of leaving the room.

"It doesn't matter. Nope. No way. You're not letting me off the hook that easy," Kimmy said. "You've got to let me make it up to you somehow."

Molly walked over and hit the On button on the PowerBook that Barbara had bought her at the start of the school year. Hoping that Kimmy would take the hint that maybe, just possibly, there might be something like homework about to break out here any second.

Not a chance.

"Well," Kimmy said, continuing to hold up her end of a conversation only she was really having, "I owe you one."

"Deal. We'll come up with something, I promise."

Now, please just . . . *go.*

Molly just wanted to talk to Sam.

"Soooooo," Kimmy said, "now that that's out of the way, tell me *everything* about the insanely cute Josh Cameron."

Molly sighed and turned down the sound on her computer, wishing there was a button like that for Kimberly Anne Evans sometimes.

Molly said it was pretty much the way she'd explained it to Barbara, that she just went up there to tell Josh Cameron face-to-face about Jen Parker dying.

"Nothing more to tell," she said.

Kimmy wasn't buying it. "There has to be more to it than that."

"Why?" Molly said.

"Are you sure you don't have some kind of, like, secret motive for wanting to meet him?"

Molly turned back around toward her computer, as if making sure she'd turned it off. Just so Kimmy couldn't see her face. Sometimes Kimmy talked so much, she made you forget that she didn't miss much around 1A Joyless Street.

Could she possibly know?

Molly casually opened the middle drawer of her desk. The blue metal box—with the lock on it—was still there. The box that contained the letters her mom had written Molly the last month of her life.

Now she turned back around. "A secret motive? What does that mean?"

"I mean, you could have sent him a letter. Or gotten some kind of e-mail address."

"Right. I'm sure e-mails get through to him right away, no problem. He's probably checking his mail constantly."

"Oh, come on. There are ways you could have gotten the message to him."

Molly said, "Like I said, I wanted to talk to him in person. Really talk to him. My mom said it's the way people used to do it before all they had to do was push the Send button."

"I guess that's the part I'm not getting," Kimmy said.

Stuck on this now, probably forever.

"I mean, I know what you told my mom. But what made this such a life-and-death thing all of a sudden?"

It was a dumb enough thing to say that even Kimmy realized it as soon as it was out of her mouth, like something she had spilled all over the bed.

"Sorry," she said.

"No problem."

"All I'm saying is, Josh Cameron and your mom hadn't seen each other since college. That's what my mom said. They broke up, your mom went off to London, end of story. It was, what, twelve years ago?"

"Something like that," Molly said.

"So how come you thought this news about your mom—as awful as it is—was suddenly, like, something he *had* to know?"

Molly had figured out in just a few months how important it was for Kimmy to know stuff. Even the silliest stuff about Molly, about school. About Sam, whom she didn't even like.

But there was no way she could know the truth about Josh Cameron. Sam had scared Molly about how easy it was for people to hack into your e-mail if they knew how. Just one of those things he knew that most kids their age didn't. The only time they ever talked about Josh was either in person or on their cells, and even then they never used his name. So there was no extension Kimmy could have been listening on. And Molly was always ridiculously careful to have her door closed when she and Sam were talking on the phone.

This had to be just a fishing expedition, in the constant fishing expedition about other people that was Kimmy's life. It seemed to make her crazy that Molly didn't share every single detail the way Kimmy did, every single day.

"Your mom must have told you that Josh and my mom really were like this great romance," Molly said. "Like in a movie. First love for both of them and all like that. Come on. Adults say all the time you never forget your first love."

"Even if you're Josh Cameron? The world's most eligible?"

"Well, I thought it was worth it," Molly said. She'd had enough. "And now, Miss Kimberly, I've got to get some homework done before I get the old hammer dropped on me."

"What was he like?"

Sigh. Getting rid of Kimmy was like telling the wind not to blow.

Maybe if Molly gave her what she wanted, she'd leave.

"What was who like?" she said. "Josh?"

Kimmy said, "No, the new substitute teacher in English. Yes, Josh, you goose."

"He was cool," Molly said.

"Cuter in person?"

"Yes," Molly said. "I thought only contact lenses could make your eyes that blue."

35

Do the girl thing.

"I can't believe you got to meet him before I did."

"Not in any kind of way you'd ever want to, though," Molly said.

"You know how much I love the Celtics," Kimmy said.

"Not the Celtics, Kimmy. Just one particular Celtic. Him."

Molly suspected that if you pinned Kimmy down, she couldn't tell you whether a basketball was blown up or stuffed. But it was true that she did have a huge crush on Josh Cameron. That was the weird coincidence here, something Molly had never considered. There were more pictures of Josh Cameron on Kimmy's walls than of Orlando Bloom. Or the guy from the last *Star Wars* movie, whose name Molly could never remember.

"If you tell me everything he said, I'll let you do your homework," Kimmy said.

Molly made most of it up.

Made him the Josh Cameron she'd hoped to meet.

If only. . . .

CHAPTER 6

$\mathcal{M}$olly and Sam were having lunch in the cafeteria. Macaroni and cheese. Molly thought it was thicker than usual and an orange color she wasn't all that comfortable with, so her portion had been piled on top of Sam's even before he said what he said at pretty much any meal they shared.

"You gonna finish that?"

Instead he said, "There's something I want to show you."

"Do *not* open your mouth and play 'Hey, look!' when you are eating my macaroni and whatever that is," Molly said.

"I would never do something like that," Sam said.

"I'm warning you, Sam Bloom. This time I really will get up and leave this table."

As usual, they had found a couple of seats at the end of one of the long tables near the window. Just the two of them. Like a secret society of two. More secret than ever, these days.

Sam reached into his pocket, then pressed his hand to his chest so she couldn't see what he'd brought out.

"Is this another card trick? I know all your card tricks."

Molly wanted to add, And how you do them.

But she didn't. If there was one true foundation to their friendship, other than loyalty, it was this: Molly let Sam Bloom think he was smarter than she was.

"You don't know all of them," he said. "Or how I do them, even if you think you do."

Molly said, "Stop that."

"What?"

"Reading my mind."

"Can't," he said. "It's like reading one of my all-time favorite books."

He put his hand on the table between them, and when he took it away, it was a kind of magic trick.

Because there were two tickets to the Celtics opener. At the TD Banknorth Garden. Tonight.

Molly stared at the tickets, back at Sam, then back at the tickets. "*No . . . way,*" she said. "No bloody way."

"Bloody?" Sam said. "I thought we had gotten rid of all the Buckingham Palace in you, milady."

"You're the one who keeps telling me I'm a work in progress," she said. She pointed to the tickets, almost like she was afraid to touch them, like she was afraid if she did they'd disappear. "How come you didn't tell me last night you had these tickets, you loser?"

"You're calling me a loo-zar when I have just presented you with two tickets to basketball heaven?"

"Good point," Molly said. "Okay, how'd you get them?"

"My mom trains the assistant to the president of the team, I forget her name," he said. "Robin somebody."

"And she gave your mom these tickets, and she gave them to you, and . . . we're going?"

"No, Mols, I just wanted to show you the tickets. I'm actually going to *ask* Kimmy."

Then he put up his hand and leaned across the table a little so Molly could give him a high-five.

"Anyway," he said, "the fact that we're going is the bad news."

"The bad news?"

He nodded. She knew he was playing with her now. It was understood that he just had to do that whenever he could and that she just had to go along. Just because it made him so happy.

"Okay, I'll bite," she said. "What's the good news?"

"Well," Sam said, "I suppose you could look at it as good news. Some people would look at it that way . . . the news, I mean . . . that we are also allowed to show up early tonight and go into the Celtics locker room and hang with the players for a few minutes after they're dressed."

Now Sam was the one who looked amazed. Looking at her like she wasn't giving him the reaction he'd expected.

Maybe like the happy winner on one of his dopey game shows.

"Mols, work with me here. Locker room. Is there a problem?"

Molly said, "What am I going to say to him once we're in there? 'Hey, Dad, me again. Where should I wait for you after the game?' "

"No," Sam said, "I don't think that's the way I'd go. But we've got all day to figure out how we want to play it."

"This is a bad idea."

"Now who's the loo-zar? This is a *great* idea."

"And I'm not going to get to go, anyway," she said. "I happen to be grounded, remember?"

Sam looked at his watch. "We've only got a couple of minutes before we have to go to English," he said. "So do you want to mope about what you're going to say to Mr. Wonderful once we get into the locker room, or that you don't think we can get you out of jail?"

"Jail," she said. "My groundedness."

Sam said, "Good, on account of that's the easy one. I'll have my mom call Barbara. Nobody ever says no to their trainer. They're afraid they'll be punished the next time in the gym."

"Fine," Molly said.

"Control yourself, girl."

"Let's say I do get out of jail for the night. How does it help if I get to see somebody today who didn't want to see me yesterday?"

"He won't run away this time."

"Why not?"

"He just won't."

Across the room, Molly noticed Kimmy with some of her bubbleheaded friends, some of whom talked even more than she did. If such a thing was possible.

Kimmy waved.

Molly waved.

Sam said, "You didn't ask me who's taking us to the game."

"Who *is* taking us to the game?"

"Uncle Adam."

"Uncle Adam the sportswriter?"

"No," Sam said, because he couldn't help himself. "Uncle Adam from the X-Men."

"And that's going to help us?"

"Think about it, Mols," Sam said.

Molly smiled. She imagined a cartoon lightbulb above her head. "Josh Cameron will see me walk into the locker room with a reporter."

Sam nodded.

Molly said, "And he'll be afraid I might spill the beans?"

"Boston baked beans, girlfriend."

"So I get his attention—then what?"

"You ask to talk to him alone. And you tell him again that you're telling the truth. And if he doesn't believe you then, well, we may have to go sniffle-sniffle on him and say that if he won't believe you, maybe Adam Burke from the Boston stinking *Globe* will."

"That almost sounds like blackmail," Molly said.

"Doesn't sound like," Sam said. "Is."

He put his hand across the table for a real handshake now. Molly obliged.

"It's on," she said.

Barbara caved.

Said Molly could go to the game. Told how persuasive her dear friend Emma Bloom had been on the phone as she made the case that Molly just had to be allowed to go—how many chances does a person get to go to an opening night game *and* meet the players? Emma had even said that Barbara was the one who deserved to be grounded if she didn't let Molly go.

41

Sam's mom could apparently lay it on as thick as Sam did when he really wanted something from somebody.

"Anyway," Barbara said. "Bill's on his way to Los Angeles today. When he gets there, I'll just explain my position."

Barbara's position: While nothing had changed from the day before, and while this *certainly* did not mean Molly could even *consider* pulling a stunt like that *ever* again, Barbara could not in good conscience prevent Molly from getting a chance like this. The chance, she said, to see her mother's old friend Josh play in person. And on opening night.

When Molly added it up, it was a tremendous opportunity for Barbara, even if her heart was in the right place. Just because all adults loved to play the part of hero.

It was win-win for everybody, if you thought about it that way.

"Nothing wrong with a little happiness in your life," Barbara said, and hugged Molly.

Molly hugged back for once.

It was Friday, but Molly said she was going upstairs anyway to do her weekend homework. Before she did, Barbara said, "Maybe next time Sam could find a way to include Kimmy?"

Molly said she'd mention that to Sam for sure.

When she got upstairs, Kimmy was in her room. It happened so often now that Molly was surprised when she walked into her room and Kimmy *wasn't* there. But since Molly never considered herself more than a houseguest, no matter how many times Barbara Evans told her she was family now, she never made an issue of it. Even though she wondered constantly what was

42

wrong with Kimmy's own room. Or what was so fascinating about Molly's.

"I heard," Kimmy said. "You are soooo lucky, girl."

She was doing her best to act happy. Before Molly could say anything, Kimmy said, "Next time I should try to get grounded."

"I'm still grounded," Molly said. "Just not tonight."

That's all Kimmy had today. One of her shortest room visits on record.

"Say hi to Josh," she said, then added, "your new best friend."

Molly knew a lot about the TD Banknorth Garden, which was the new name for the Fleet Center, which was the new Boston Garden really, since the old one had been torn down.

"That was the one known as the Gah-den," Sam said, exaggerating a Boston accent.

Molly knew that the basketball court here, the one known as the "parquet floor" because of its design, with all the squares in it, looked exactly like the one at the old Gah-den.

Part of all the things she had learned since she had learned that Josh Cameron was her dad.

Or her un-dad.

That was probably more accurate, considering the way things had gone yesterday.

"The old Celtics won all their championships at the old Garden," she said.

"Thanks," he said. "I wasn't aware of that."

"This isn't like a spelling bee," she said. "It's not me against you for who knows more about the Celtics."

"Spell *parquet*," he said.

"Ha ha."

"I used to go to the old Garden," he said. "What a dump."

"Oh, please," Molly said. "You're too young to remember."

"I've told you before," Sam said. "I remember the *womb*."

Which Molly had to admit was probably true.

Adam Burke, Sam's uncle, looked more like a college kid than some of the sportswriters Sam liked to watch yell at each other on television. Long hair that always seemed to look messy, jeans, blue blazer, white shirt. Penny loafers. He had told them on the ride over that because it was the first game of the season for the Celtics, he was working tonight, which meant he'd have to write after the game. But he'd arranged it with the Celtics public relations people that Molly and Sam could wait for him in the press lounge if they promised to behave.

"Okay," Sam said. "We promise not to make fun of the other sportswriters."

"No matter what," Molly said.

"Even if they try to impress us when they're not trying to impress each other," Sam said.

"No matter what," Molly said.

"How lucky am I," Adam Burke said, "to get to go to the opener with the two funniest twelve-year-olds in the greater Boston area?"

"At least you appreciate that," Sam said.

Sam had to get the last word in, even with adults.

They had arrived at the TD Banknorth Garden early. All the gold-colored seats were still empty; some girl singer Molly didn't recognize was practicing the national anthem. Then Adam Burke took them to the Sports Museum that was inside the new Garden, and to the small television studio where some of the Celtics announcers did their pregame and postgame shows. When they came back to the arena, Adam Burke pointed out the championship banners hanging from the ceiling and all the retired numbers belonging to the great olden-days Celtics players.

"The next one to go up there, once he retires, will be Josh Cameron's number three," he said. "But if he retires, that means he'll have gotten old, which nobody around here expects to happen."

Then he said he was going to the locker room to interview some of the Celtics players for the column he had to write before they even played the game, just to hold the space in the early edition of the *Globe*.

"Don't even try to understand," Adam said. "It's never made any sense to me, either."

He left them in their second-row seats while some of the Celtics showed up on the court in their warm-up clothes and began to shoot around.

Up close, like this, they were the biggest human beings Molly Parker had ever seen in her life.

"I feel like we're in *Jurassic Park*," she whispered to Sam. "We don't grow them this big in London. Why is that?"

"I don't know."

"I thought you knew everything."

"Not everything," he said. "Just more than most people."

Molly squeezed his hand, which always made him blush. "Lucky for me," she said.

Sam couldn't play sports to save his life. Couldn't throw a

football or catch one or make a basket in gym. But he knew so much about sports, the Boston sports teams in particular, it was as if all the information stored inside his head did make him some kind of unofficial jock.

Or maybe just the jock he secretly wanted to be.

When he'd stopped telling Molly who the players were and where they went to college, Molly said, "He probably won't even remember me."

"He'll remember you. Trust me." Sam looked at her. "You bring your mom's letter?"

"It's in my pocket. Not that it did me much good yesterday."

"Good," he said. "Now we just have to hope he's in the locker room when we get to go in there and not hiding in the players' lounge."

Josh Cameron wasn't in the locker room. Sam whispered the names of the guys who were there, as if he were taking attendance. Teddy Wright, L. J. Brown, Nick Tutts. The PR man quickly moved Molly and Sam from one guy to the next, then got them out of there.

But no Josh.

"Now what?" Sam said when they were back outside, having met the handful of players who were in front of their lockers. "Plan B was you handing him the letter."

"I've got another plan," Molly said.

Sam said, "Oh, goody."

"Plan C," Molly said.

Then she told him what the C stood for.

CHAPTER 7

*E*ver since she had learned the truth about Josh Cameron, Molly had taken an interest in basketball.

She would even go into the closet and find Mr. Evans's basketball sometimes and spin it in her hands while she thought about what her life might be like if Josh knew about her.

But for the most part, basketball was still pretty much a mystery to her.

She had to admit that she knew a lot more about soccer—they called it football in England—and even cricket, just because you had to over there if you cared at all about sports, except for the kids who'd just arrived at the American School of London from the States, chattering about basketball and baseball and football and everything *except* soccer and cricket.

So most of her first live NBA game was a blur, except for this: Even a total idiot could see that what Josh Cameron was doing on the court was different from what everybody else could do.

Nine other players out there. Three officials. All these people around him, Molly thought, and it's as if he's still all by himself, which is the way her mom had said it always was with him.

Josh World, she had called it.

It was exciting when you saw it this close, but it made her sad, too, something she tried to explain to Sam at halftime.

"It really is like he's in a world of his own," she said.

"Your point being?"

"I've got about as much a chance of breaking into it, getting him to do something he doesn't want to do, as all those guys trying to guard him."

"But that's the thing about basketball," Sam said. "He *needs* those other guys."

He was eating again. Had been eating since the game started. Popcorn. Two hot dogs. Ice cream. Now some nacho thing with cheese the same yucky color as the cheese of the macaroni and cheese at school. Like the Celtics against the 76ers was really just an all-you-can-eat contest.

Sam said, "It's the kind of player he is. He's only great when he's making the people around him great. You get that part, right?"

"I guess so."

"Nah, Mols. You know so. Those other guys round him out as a player. That's what Uncle Adam always writes about him. And just about everybody else, too. You've got to convince Mr. Wonderful that you can basically do the same thing, just off the court. You and him, a better team."

Molly grabbed one of his chips, making sure there was no cheese on it. "Are you absolutely sure you're only twelve years old?" she said.

Sam kept eating. "The guy is going to love you once he gets to know you," Sam said. "Now he's got to get to know you."

48

"Fat chance."

Sam ignored her, saying, "And if he gets to know you and doesn't love you, then he is a total, screaming moron."

The Celtics finally ended up with the ball with twenty seconds left, and the game tied. Their coach called what Sam said was their last timeout, even if it seemed both teams had been calling one timeout after another for the last hour or so. Molly checked out the players huddling around the coach, but could see that he wasn't the one doing the talking.

Josh Cameron was.

Molly tried to compare this Josh to the one who seemed so scared of her when he got into his car and drove off, but couldn't do it.

Over all the noise of the crowd, Sam shouted, "He likes to dribble out most of the clock and then do something amazing to win the game."

They were standing on their chairs because everybody else at the TD Banknorth Garden was standing, getting ready for the last play.

"Just watch," Sam said.

But she had been watching every move Josh Cameron made all night long.

They passed the ball in to him at half-court. At first, he didn't even dribble. Just stood there in this cool way, like he knew something that no one else in this loud, crazy place knew, looking up at the clock over the Celtics basket.

Twelve seconds.

Ten.

Now six.

He made his move then, beating the man guarding him with his very first dribble, flying past him, looking as if he were on his way to the basket, ready to go up against the 76ers' biggest guys once more, ready to beat them and the clock at the same time.

Only he didn't drive, seeing that the 76ers had cut him off. Instead he stopped about ten feet from the basket, doing that even though he'd been going at full speed. Put the brakes on so hard, Molly half-expected to hear the screech of car tires.

She was sure he was going to make the kind of jump shot he'd been making the whole game every time he pulled up like this.

Three seconds left.

He went up into the air.

He was going to do it!

Somehow Molly had forgotten how mad she was at him. She was as excited as everyone else now.

Josh released the ball then, and Molly's heart sank, because she had a perfect angle to see that his shot wasn't going to be anywhere near the basket. It was off. Off to the left.

Which is where L. J. Brown, one of the Celtics' biggest guys, was already in midair, in perfect position to catch what wasn't a shot at all from Josh Cameron because it was a pass, a perfect pass.

L. J. Brown caught it and dunked it in the same motion as the horn sounded.

The Celtics, even the ones on the bench, came rushing out to mob Brown. Molly kept watching Josh, who was smiling at the scene from where he'd thrown Brown the ball, smiling and nodding his head. Then he turned away from the celebration under the basket and walked past the Celtics bench, right past where Molly and Sam were sitting, and disappeared down the runway that led to the locker room.

Even now, nobody could touch him.

Molly grabbed Sam by the arm and said, "Come on, we've got to go."

"The game just ended," Sam said. "You can tell. See all the happy people around us?"

"Come *on*," Molly said. "Time for Plan C."

"This is a really bad idea," Sam said.

"It's a great idea, and you know it. You just don't like it because you didn't come up with it."

"We're supposed to wait in the press lounge."

"You'll be back there before you know it."

"Plan C," Sam said, shaking his head sadly, even as Molly kept pulling him through the crowd and telling him not to worry. "If I were grading it honestly, I'd actually give it a D or an F."

Molly knew that where the Celtics players parked their cars for games at the TD Banknorth Garden was next door, where the old Garden had been until they tore it down. Sam said that was the kind of thing *he* was supposed to know and not her. Molly said she'd read it in one of Uncle Adam's columns, even before she'd met Sam. It was when she had first started to read up on Josh Cameron, after her mom had finally told her the truth. Adam Burke had written about standing over there with Josh Cameron—would she ever be able to start thinking of him as her dad?—right before the playoffs the year before, asking him if he ever ran into any Celtics ghosts in the area.

"Only if they're driving Hummers," Josh Cameron had joked.

Then Adam Burke had written that the new Celtics had Josh Cameron, so they didn't need any ghosts, even if trying to guard him was like trying to catch one.

Molly was the one who really remembered everything, not Sam. *She* was the one who remembered the womb.

"We're never going to find this place in the dark," Sam said.

"Oh, I bet they have lights for the players and everything," Molly said.

"One of these days I'm going to have to learn how to say no to you."

Molly said, "Just follow me and start thinking of what you're going to say to him."

"I'm getting hungry," Sam said.

It made her giggle. Even in the middle of an adventure, Sam thought a quick snack could fix everything.

And this was an adventure, even more than yesterday's was. But it just had to work. Had to. It wasn't as if she could keep coming up with new and different ways to run into just about the most famous athlete in America every single day.

"You're absolutely sure you know where we're going?" Sam said.

Molly had let go of him by now and was walking about twenty feet ahead. Without looking back, she windmilled her arm at him. "Just pick up the pace."

"*Do* you know where you're going?"

"Sort of."

She was guessing what exit to use, but by now she had no bearings. So when they went out what she was hoping would be a back door, they found themselves in the middle of all the people and all the postgame excitement of Causeway Street.

Molly told herself not to panic, they still had plenty of time. That's why she'd rushed Sam out of the arena as soon as Josh Cameron had made his pass.

"The old Garden had to be this way, right?" she said.

"Left, actually," Sam said.

"You know what I meant."

"Right."

They both laughed, being silly for a moment. It seemed to make Sam less scared. He preferred to have his adventures inside his head. It was different with Molly. Maybe because the worst thing that could happen to her had already happened . . . .

She wasn't scared now, just determined to make this work.

They made their way up the sidewalk, picked an alley, found out it was a dead end. Sam said, "I'm trying to picture the way it used to be here," and then told her they should keep going. They finally came to a small street that took them back behind Causeway Street and to the protected lot that Sam said was exactly where the old Gah-den had been.

"Has to be it," Molly said. "Those are the same cars I saw yesterday."

There was a security guard where the players would probably walk through a small entrance into the fenced-off area, and another guard at a bigger entrance where it looked like they would drive out. Molly also noticed that it was the brightest area back here, as bright as day.

Not good.

"We are never going to get in there," Sam said.

"Think positively," she said. "Isn't that what you're always telling me?"

"Yeah," he said. "In social studies."

"Are you ready?" Molly said.

"Not really."

"Start sniffling," Molly said.

Molly couldn't hear everything he was saying to the guard, but knew basically what he was supposed to say as she was sneaking along the outside of the fence, over by where she assumed the cars would drive out of the lot.

Only when Sam raised his voice did she hear him saying, "I'll never find my sister, never, never, *never*!"

She couldn't hear what the guard said, then she heard Sam say, "This has to be parking lot B. That's where we said we'd meet if we got separated."

Then he ran—or what passed for running for him—away from the first guard and around the chain-link fence to where the second guard was. The one who was closest to Molly. The first guard chased him, and the second guard came out to stop him, and when he did, Molly, staying low, got through the entrance and behind the first car she came to, which was a Mercedes.

The first guard went back to his post, telling the second guard the "fast showerers" would be showing up any second. Molly could hear the second guard say for Sam to stay right where he was, he'd left his cell phone inside his booth.

Huge break.

As soon as the guard turned around, Sam Bloom made what Molly was sure was the quickest move of his whole life, maybe because he didn't have to go far, and joined Molly behind the Mercedes.

The next thing they heard was the guard saying, "Crazy kids."

He had that right, she had to admit.

According to Sam's watch, they waited for an hour.

A lot of Celtics players had arrived in the lot by then and driven off. Molly and Sam had slowly moved behind the cars, toward where they could see Josh Cameron's Navigator. It also gave them a better look at the arriving players, Sam announcing their names to Molly in a whisper, as if he were a PA announcer introducing them before the game.

"Terry Thompson."

"Teddy."

"Nick."

"Antonio."

"L.J."

Molly said, "I *know* that's L.J. He just won the game."

"No need to snap at me," Sam said.

It was past eleven o'clock now.

Sam said, "Uncle Adam's going to be finishing his column soon, and then he's going to come get us in the lounge, only we're not going to be there."

"Will he call your cell?"

"Probably," Sam said. "I'll just explain that we're in the players' lot hiding out by Cameron's car."

"Hey," Molly said, "why do you think I called it Plan C? Cameron's car. All Cs."

"That's great, Mols. No kidding. I can't tell you how impressed I am."

Then Molly told him to hush, here came Josh Cameron now.

He was carrying the same bag he'd had with him the day before. Wearing the same leather jacket and a yellow baseball cap.

"Way to go, J.C.," the first guard said.

"It's all good," Josh Cameron said.

Molly and Sam both jumped when he did the remote thing and they heard the doors unlock and the car engine start.

"Well, that scared the—" Sam said.

Molly whispered, "You don't have time to be scared. You're on."

"You didn't tell me acting would be this much work."

He didn't move, though. Just stayed where he was, crouched down. Molly had to admit he did look a little like a frog in that pose.

"Go," Molly said. "Before he drives off on me again."

And just like that, like the car alarm that had gone off a few minutes before when Terry Thompson, the backup point guard, had hit the wrong button on his own remote, Sam Bloom said, "Oh my God . . . Josh CAMERON!" Walking around from the back of the Navigator to the driver's side.

"Good grief, kid, you nearly scared the—" Josh Cameron stopped himself right there. "What do you think you're doing out here at this time of night?"

In the distance, Molly could hear the guard say, "Aw, man, I'm sorry, J.C. That kid gave me some story about his sister a while ago and musta snuck by me."

"I got it, Bob," Josh said. "No worries."

"Don't make me go yet," Sam said. "I have been waiting sooooo long for you."

He sounded like Kimmy, Molly thought.

"It's official," Josh said. "I am now going for the record of kids sneaking up on me in parking lots this week."

Like he was talking to himself.

"I didn't mean to sneak up on you like this," Sam said. "But I'm your biggest fan, and you've got to sign something for me. Please!"

That was Molly's cue.

"Please please please!" Sam said.

She opened the door and climbed into the backseat and, as quietly as she could, as quietly as anybody ever could, shut the door behind her.

She got her eyes just above the window, saw that Josh's back was to her, and then dove into the way-back of his Navigator.

Her ride home.

CHAPTER 8

*T*he papers always just said that Josh Cameron lived somewhere in the Back Bay section of Boston, which Molly knew covered a lot of territory. Nobody ever mentioned the street he lived on, not even on any of the Web sites devoted exclusively to him.

The best one, the one where Molly got a lot of her information and found out what his biggest fans were saying about him, was called SonsofCameron.com. It was modeled after a cool Red Sox site that Sam had shown her called SonsofSamHorn.com, which was named after a former Red Sox first baseman who now did some television for them and had fan postings so funny, they would make Molly and Sam laugh out loud.

SonsofCameron.com wasn't as funny, but every time Molly went to it, she thought the same thing: Daughter of Cameron, checking in.

But even they wouldn't talk about his exact address, treating it like some kind of state secret. Out of respect for the Man, the people running the site would write from time to time when somebody asked where Josh lived. For all Molly knew, Josh

Cameron could have been living around the corner from the Evanses.

So she didn't know where they were going. She just stayed low, bumping along, hoping he was going straight home, wherever home was, and not out on a date for the rest of the night.

Sam was the one who had brought up the date angle.

"What happens," he'd said during the game, "if he's meeting one of his girlfriends somewhere? Or picking her up?"

"Girl*friend*," Molly had said, correcting him. "He's dating the girl from *Worth Avenue*." It was a new TV show on FOX. "The icky Amanda Ross. And they're shooting right now in Hollywood, I read it on SonsofCameron."

"Mols," Sam had said, "I know I have to watch what I say about Mr. Wonderful, but I have a feeling she's not the only one he's dating. So, what if he goes out on a date tonight?"

Molly'd said, "Nobody ever said it was a perfect plan, Sam."

Please be going straight home, she kept thinking now, even though it was hard to hear herself think the way he had U2 blaring on what she had to admit was a pretty amazing sound system. So amazing that Molly couldn't tell sometimes whether it was the thump of the bass she was hearing, or herself banging against the backseat.

Somehow over the music, she heard his cell phone go off.

He turned down the music.

"Hey," he said.

Then, "Yeah, I guess it was a pretty cool way to start the season."

Then, "Another day at the office."

59

Another day at the office?

"I miss you, too, baby."

Had to be the icky Amanda.

Then he talked to her about her show for a few minutes, though he didn't sound all that interested to Molly. Said he'd see her in a couple of weeks. Said he missed her.

Finally, "I love you, too, baby."

He loved *her*?

Not possible, according to Molly's mom, who said he'd never really loved anybody.

They were going faster now, Molly getting thrown around even more on the curves, wondering if maybe there was one speed limit for Josh Cameron and another for everybody else. When he really gunned the Navigator into one turn—what was this, the Boston version of the Grand Prix?—Molly went hard into the side of the car, bumping her head.

Hard.

She couldn't help herself. It made her yell out, "Ow!"

With the music still down, it was Molly who must have sounded like a car alarm now.

The car swerved, throwing Molly into the opposite inside wall of the car.

"What the—" Josh Cameron yelled. "Who's back there?"

Somehow he got the car under control, slowing it down.

"Who's back there?" he repeated.

No reason to hide anymore. Molly poked her head above the seat in front of her and could see him trying to drive the car and look in his rearview mirror at the same time.

Molly stared at the eyes looking at her from the mirror now.

He didn't look happy.

She smiled anyway.

"Me again," she said.

"Stowaway brat causes Cameron to lose control of car on Storrow Drive," he said to himself. He was angry this time. "The media would have had a field day with that one."

Molly stayed where she was in the way-back, afraid to get any closer to him.

He was still talking to himself, looking at the road in front of him mostly, but occasionally using the mirror to look right at Molly with a mean face.

"Twelve years in the league," he said. "I go up against Shaq. Don't get hurt. Ewing. Hakeem. Don't get hurt. Now I almost get taken out by a pushy twelve-year-old *girl*."

"Sorry," Molly said, her voice sounding squeaky, the way it did when she got nervous, not knowing what else to say at the moment.

"I don't even want to know what you think you're doing, kid," he said. "I thought we said all we had to say yesterday. I ought to call the police and let them handle this, but I'm not going to. Just tell me where Barbara lives, and I'll take you home."

Molly didn't say anything.

"Hey," he said. "I asked you a question."

It made Molly think of a question of her own.

This jerk is my father?

But she had come this far. She was going to say what she needed to say to him.

"We didn't finish our conversation yesterday," she said.

He pulled the car over. Molly could see they were on Commonwealth Ave. now, the part between Kenmore Square and the Public Garden, a little park and biking path separating the eastbound and westbound traffic. Josh Cameron turned around and looked at her. For some reason she noticed his cap, which read "Dan Bailey, Livingston, Montana."

"No, that's where you're wrong, we *did* finish our conversation," he said. "Maybe you didn't. But I did. It was a nice try on your part. And this is an even nicer try tonight. We need some of the guys off our bench to try as hard as you do."

Molly rubbed the place where she'd hit her head. She could feel the bump. Josh Cameron hadn't even asked if she was all right.

Molly said, "You don't believe me because you don't want to believe me."

He whipped off his cap then and threw it down on the backseat.

"This is getting annoying," he said.

Tell me about it, she thought.

"Here's what I believe," he said. "I believe you're Jen's daughter. I do. I believe she came up with a story about me being your dad, to explain why she ran off to Europe and never came back. I don't know, maybe she thought there'd be some money in it after she was gone."

"It wasn't like that," Molly said.

"But what I don't believe is some sneaky kid off the street showing up out of the blue and telling me I'm her father. And what I don't like is that kid hiding out in my car and nearly causing a stinking accident on my way home from the game."

"I had to see you again," Molly said.

Standing her ground, even though she was sitting down.

"For the last time," he said, "either tell me where you live, or I'm going to drive around the corner to the Ritz, where I happen to be living right now, hand you over to the concierge, and have him deal with you."

All that work getting to practice, Molly thought. And he was right around the corner after all.

Then she held up the envelope. "She wrote it all down in this letter to me, once she knew I was Googling you on my own. She said I should know the real you and not the one in the newspaper and in magazines."

"A letter," Josh said.

"My mom wrote a bunch of letters the last couple of months," Molly said.

She swallowed hard now, knowing she couldn't cry in front of him but wanting to cry the way she did every single time she pictured Jen Parker in bed, propped up in front of all her pillows, her laptop actually on her lap, typing away. Her mom, who had dreamed about being a figure skater when she was Molly's age, who had been a good enough athlete and a good enough skater and a hard enough worker to have that dream, wasting away before Molly's eyes, like she was shrinking into herself.

"They're about all kinds of stuff," she said. "Stuff that's already happened. Stuff she thinks is *going* to happen to me as I get older. This one just happens to be about you."

She figured that would get his attention. Mom had said it always had to be about him.

She went for it now.

"You give me fifteen minutes," she said, "I'll let you read it."

"You sound like my agent."

Molly said, "I didn't know I'd have to."

She wasn't usually this sarcastic with anybody, particularly adults, but there was something about him that brought it out in her.

"You've got a smart mouth," he said. "I wonder where you get that from?"

"My mom," Molly said. "But just the smart part."

CHAPTER 9

*H*e didn't actually live in the hotel part of the old Ritz-Carlton Hotel on Arlington Street. It turned out that there was a side of the Ritz made up of apartments, the awning in front reading "Two Commonwealth." Josh Cameron pulled up to that door in the Navigator, got out on the street side, handed the parking guy his keys.

Molly climbed into the regular backseat and got out of the car on the street side.

The parking guy didn't notice her at first. He was talking to Josh as the two of them came around toward the entrance.

"We're goin' all the way again, Mr. C," he said.

"Why the heck not, Lindsay?" Josh said.

Lindsay, in his cap and gray overcoat that had "Ritz-Carlton" written on the front, noticed Molly then.

"This pretty little girl with you, Mr. C?"

"Yeah," he said, even though it sounded like more of a grunt to Molly.

"What's your name, pretty girl?"

"Molly."

"And what's your relation to the world's greatest hooper?"

Before Molly could say anything, Josh Cameron said, "Niece."

Niece, Molly thought.

Nice.

Then an amazing thing happened, even though she knew Josh was doing it just to get her inside. He took her by the hand.

It wasn't the way Molly thought it would be. Or had hoped it would be.

Still, she held her father's hand for the first time in her life.

The apartment, with its view of the park and the lights of the city all around it, was at the penthouse level.

But Molly thought the best view was inside Josh's apartment, not what you saw when you looked out. The longest sofa she had ever seen in her life. The widest television screen. The thickest carpet.

Some of the biggest trophies.

She didn't ask why he was living here, but he told her when they got inside.

"I moved over here while I'm having my townhouse renovated," he said. "Lock, stock, and Mattie."

Molly said, "Is Mattie your dog?"

"Nah, even if she treats me like a dog sometimes," he said. "Mattie is my live-in housekeeper, day planner, den mother. I'd call her my unofficial grandmother, but she's not nice enough to be a grandmother."

"Why do you keep her around?" Molly said.

"Because she's indispensable," he said.

"Fascinating," Molly said.

She couldn't help herself.

"More sarcasm?"

"You bring it out of me."

"Your mother used to make everything my fault, too," he said. "Why don't you just give me the letter, before your fifteen minutes are up."

Molly didn't care how crabby he sounded, she had at least made it from the game to his car to here.

"The kitchen's that way, if you want something to drink," he said.

"I'm fine."

She sat down on the long sofa, which was so soft she was afraid she would disappear inside it. It was like she'd sat on some kind of cloud up at the top of the Ritz.

Josh Cameron held out his hand, as if asking her to give back something she'd swiped. "The letter."

She stood up, walked over, and handed it to him. He handed her the remote for the television set. "Watch TV if you don't want something to drink. Or check out the view. I'll be back in a few."

He left her in the living room by herself, wondering how many other rooms there were in this place, wondering what Kimmy Evans would say if she knew where Molly was right now.

She thought about calling Sam, but the only thing to tell him at this point was that she was sitting here in Josh Cameron's living room. So she turned on the television, volume down way low, and found the New England Sports Network channel— NESN, as it was known in Boston—and watched the highlights of the Celtics game. For the second time tonight, she saw him doing all the amazing things he'd done to the 76ers. Some of

67

them she felt as if she were watching for the first time, like she'd missed them the first time around, even though she'd been just twenty feet away.

When the woman talking about Josh and the Celtics started showing highlights of other games, she thought about her mom's letter.

She knew what was in it. Knew practically by heart because she'd read it so many times.

Her mom told more in that letter—or maybe just told it better—than she'd ever told Molly about Josh. She started from the time they first met in the bookstore at UConn. She'd asked what a jock was doing in a bookstore, and he'd told her, "I'm not like the other ones. I'm more than a jock." And how she'd believed that for the longest time, until she began to figure out that he had settled for being a jock because that was the easiest way for him, that was the world he could control.

She kept loving him anyway, even as she felt him slipping away from her, telling her the whole while that he loved her as much as she loved him. As much as he loved basketball.

She finally decided that he would never love anything as much as he loved basketball. Or himself. Or at least the self, her mom wrote, that the world knew.

There was a lot more to it than that.

Later, she found out she was going to have a baby. She never considered telling him, because she could tell by then that a wife and a baby didn't fit his plan—or his image—because his only plan involved the National Basketball Association.

Her mom's parents were both dead by then. She had been planning for junior year abroad, anyway, had given up on Josh

68

Cameron asking her not to go. So she went. She went and took the money she had inherited from her own mom and dad and fell in love with London and never came home.

Jen Parker said that she had planned to tell Molly the whole truth someday, when she was older. Maybe when Molly had become the college girl. But then Jen became sick. By that point Molly had actually figured some things out on her own, even though she didn't know the real surprise until Jen told her, the day she finally admitted that the other dad was made up.

"Sometimes I would tell myself," her mom wrote, "that Josh couldn't help loving you if he got to know you, even if he's always thought all the love in the world should be directed at him."

She was watching a taped interview with Josh Cameron when the real thing walked back into the room.

It occurred to her that the Josh she was watching on television was the one she had hoped to meet yesterday, and the one she was still hoping to meet today, even knowing what her mom had told her about him.

It was the Josh Cameron everyone wanted to know and every kid wanted to be.

Then, Molly thought, you actually *did* get to know him.

He had the unfolded pages of the letter in his hand. He used them to point at the television screen.

"Turn me off," he said. "Please."

"Only because you said please."

"Sarcasm again?"

Molly said, "I'm trying to quit."

"I'm actually a good guy," he said.

69

Molly remembered a line Sam liked to use. "Well, you play one on television."

"I give people the Josh Cameron they want, is all," he said. "And it's close enough to the real me."

"Right."

"Are you going to turn the TV off?"

Molly did.

He went and sat down in the big chair across from the sofa, one that had a UConn blue blanket draped over the back of it. Gave her the big smile from the TV Josh, as if Molly were interviewing him.

"I've got to hand it to you, kid . . . *Molly*," he said. "You're good."

"You've got to hand what to me?"

"Hey, I'm paying you a compliment. You really are good."

Molly knew this was most definitely *not* good.

Josh said, "This thing sounds just like her. And you obviously remember everything she ever told you about me."

Molly looked down and saw she still had the TV remote in her hand. She wanted to point it at him now.

Get the real Josh to stop talking.

Instead she said, "You think I wrote the letter."

Not even bothering to make it into a question.

"We both know you did." He nodded. "You took what she told you and then you came up with this version of things you want to be and *voilà*! A Dear Josh letter. Though I don't come off too dear in all of it."

"My mom wrote that letter!"

Molly was yelling at him and didn't care.

"Right."

"She did!"

"You say in here that she used to say that the hardest thing for me was being honest with myself," he said. "Okay. I'll buy that. Maybe your mom was right about that. But how honest are you being, kiddo?"

Kiddo now.

Molly felt both her hands squeezing her knees now, as hard as they could. It was like he wanted her to cry. But she wasn't going to give him the satisfaction.

"Jerk," she said.

"Nah," he said. "I'm just keeping it real. One of us has to."

"What's real is that I'm your daughter," she said, yelling again. "Why don't you get that?"

"Because that's not real," he said. "No harm, no foul. You took a shot. I've actually got to hand it to you. Not many kids your age would have had the guts to do what you've done the last couple of days."

Molly didn't know whether it was because he was making her this mad or because she felt so helpless all of a sudden. Helpless, probably. She'd had a lot of helpless in her life lately. Whatever it was—she couldn't help herself now—she felt the tears starting to come.

Even though she only ever cried when she was alone.

She wanted to say something else, but she couldn't, feeling like a jerk herself now, barely able to catch her breath, crying like a big baby.

Josh Cameron stood up. "I'll call downstairs and have them get you a cab."

Then he crumpled up the pages in his hand, made them into a ball, and fired it across the room and into a wood basket that sat next to an antique desk.

"Nothing but net," he said.

That was when Molly ran.

CHAPTER 10

When they had come into the lobby of Two Commonwealth, Josh Cameron had pointed to the door that he said opened into the lobby of the hotel part of the Ritz. When Molly came out of the elevator, she went through it, figuring that if Josh Cameron did care enough to follow her, he'd be looking for her out on the street.

For once in her life, she couldn't wait to get back to 1A Joyless Street.

Molly was brave, but not a total dope, so she wasn't going to run across the Public Garden alone at this time of night. She figured she'd go through the lobby, wait to see if the coast was clear on Arlington, then run over to Beacon and up to the corner of Beacon and Joy.

That was the plan, anyway, and she sprinted through the lobby toward the revolving doors.

"Whoa there, girl."

There was a tall young guy in a suit and a tie. Dark hair. Good-looking, Molly noticed. He was wearing a little name tag that read "Thomas O'Connor, Concierge."

"Where are you headed alone at this time of night?" he said.

"Home," she said. "I was visiting . . . a friend . . . at Two Commonwealth."

"What's the friend's name?"

Go with it, Molly thought.

Do anything just to get out of here.

"Can you keep a secret?" she said.

"It's practically the first thing they teach you at concierge school," he said.

"Josh Cameron," she said. "You can ask Lindsay the doorman. He's my uncle. Josh Cameron, I mean."

"Really?"

"Cross my heart."

"Well, why don't we call him?"

"No!"

Molly yelled at him the way she'd just yelled upstairs at good old Uncle Josh.

"He was doing an interview," Molly said, the words coming out of her like a pipe had just burst. "And I told him I'd have Lindsay call me a cab. But then I got downstairs and decided it was silly to take a cab over to Joy Street—I live on Joy Street—and, well, you got me, Mr. O'Connor."

"If Lindsay was going to call you a cab, what are you doing over on this side, then?"

"I was going to buy a candy bar, but then I remembered I forgot to ask Uncle Josh for money." She smiled and shrugged. "My bad, all the way around."

"Is Josh Cameron really your uncle?"

"Well, I think of him as my uncle. Him and my stepmom

went to college together and are still good friends, and so we've always acted as if we're related, even though technically we're not."

Somehow she managed not to gag on *stepmom.*

Molly said, "So *please* don't get me in trouble with him."

"There's still the matter of getting you home."

Molly said, "Would you mind walking me? It's really not far."

He told her to wait a second, walked over to the concierge desk, where there was another guy, older, talking on the phone.

Then Thomas O'Connor came back and said, "Let's go, kid."

Kid sounded better coming from him.

"You can call me Molly," Molly said.

As they were walking up Arlington, she told Thomas O'Connor she had to call her friend.

Sam answered on what Molly thought was half a ring.

"Where *are* you?" he whispered. "I've been, like, sick worried. You said you were going to call."

"Way home," she said. "Long story."

"Way home from where?"

"His place."

"What the heck happened?"

"Tell you at school. What happened with your uncle when he realized I was gone?"

"I told him you didn't want to wait and that he was busy, so you went home with the Hartnetts."

Stevie Hartnett's uncle was the Red Sox manager, which made him a huge celebrity at school.

"But how do you know Stevie was at the game?"

"He could have been," Sam said. There was a pause and then Sam said, "I'm under the covers, but I think my mom's coming. Quick, tell me how it went?"

"The absolute pits," she said before hanging up.

"What?" Thomas said when she put the phone away.

"What what?"

"What was the absolute pits?"

"The game."

"You got to go to the Celtics game?"

"Yeah."

"And that's a bad thing?"

"Like I told my friend, it's a long story."

"So I should stop being nosy."

"That would be good," Molly said.

She felt so tired all of a sudden, it was as if she had just played a whole basketball game herself.

When they got to Joyless Street, she pointed to show him how close 1A was to the corner. Thomas asked if she had a key, and she said she did. He said he'd wait until she was inside. She told him he didn't have to. He said it was a service that the concierge provided at the Ritz every time the concierge made a new friend.

"Nice to meet you," he said, putting out his hand.

"Same," Molly said.

At least somebody was nice to her tonight.

Molly got inside, quietly shut the big front door, and hoped Barbara was asleep on the couch, which is the way her television watching usually ended when she tried to stay up late. She liked to joke that she didn't watch David Letterman nearly as often as he watched her.

Barbara was asleep, snoring slightly, a blanket over her, the television on, a book on her chest.

Molly just left her there and tiptoed up the stairs, not wanting to wake anybody and have to lie about how getting to see the Celtics in person had been the grandest night of her entire life.

When she got inside her room, she pulled the yellow baseball cap Josh Cameron had been wearing from her back pocket, the cap she'd swiped when she got out of his car.

Sam always made fun of how much she liked those high-tech crime shows, saying that she couldn't possibly understand what they were all talking about when they were looking through their microscopes.

He was partly right.

Molly didn't actually know what DNA stood for, but she understood how it worked.

Even if all you had was somebody's hair.

to give it a shot, even though she had never played a day of organized ball in her life. So on Saturday they had gone over to City Sports on Boylston and Molly had bought her first basketball.

When Sam had asked her on the bus how tryouts had gone, she had said, "Fine."

Which wasn't entirely true.

The tryouts had been conducted during gym class. By the time they scrimmaged at the end of class, it was clear that Molly was the best one out there.

"You gonna be one of those players who carries the ball with them wherever they go?" Sam said.

"Coach said I should work on dribbling with my left hand. I'm a little weak there," she said.

"I'm the one feeling weak," Sam said.

It meant he was tired after one block. Molly never seemed to get tired. When everybody else was dragging at gym, she was still fresh. The other night, the NESN woman interviewing Josh Cameron had said something to him about how he looked fresher at the end of the game than he did at the beginning, and Molly had thought to herself, Well, maybe we have one thing in common.

"If I want exercise, I'll go to the fridge and get us a snack when we get to your house."

"It's not my house."

"Figure of speech."

Molly said, "You complain every time we make this walk."

"You'd be sad if I didn't," he said. "Admit it."

"Not as much as you think," Molly said, and laughed.

Sam made her laugh. He made her laugh even when she didn't feel like laughing, when she didn't think anything was funny or that anything would be funny ever again. Like when the subject of Josh Cameron came up.

Josh Cameron.

She wondered if she would ever think of him as her father.

By the time they made the right turn on Joy, Molly was telling Sam not to complain anymore so that he could conserve energy.

"Just let me say one more thing," he said.

"No," Molly said.

"Okay, then," he said. "Don't check out who's waiting in the alley."

Oh, my God.

Josh Cameron.

There was a small black woman with him. She had a beret on her head and a smile on her round face that almost seemed too wide for the alley where they were standing, the one you had to walk through to get to the front door at 1A Joyless. She was wearing a short topcoat and a dress underneath it and white high-topped basketball shoes. She was short and looked even shorter standing next to Josh Cameron.

To Josh the black woman said, "This her?"

Pointing at Molly, still smiling.

When he didn't say anything, she said, "This has to be her."

She walked over and started to put out her hand, then decided to give Molly a hug instead.

"I'm Mattie," she said. "The nice one in the house."

Molly pushed back from her. "Were you there the other night?"

Mattie shook her head. "I was still away, visiting my sister. Didn't get back until the next morning, and he was already off to the airport. He didn't tell me about it till today. Now here we are."

She turned around to Josh Cameron and said, "You got anything to say, now that we *are* here?"

Talking to him like she was talking to a child.

"I was just waiting for you to stop and then I was going to start."

"I'm stopped."

"Hello, Molly," Josh said.

"Ex*cuse* me?" Mattie said to him.

"Mattie," he said. "Let me do this my way. And, by the way, remind me again: Do you work for me, or do I work for you?"

Mattie turned to Molly. "Let him do things his way," she said, as if he wasn't even there. "On account of he's doing so good with you, doing things his way."

"I can actually speak for myself," Josh said.

"No," Mattie said, "you can't. Not like a normal person would speak to people. Which is why you brought me with you." Ignoring him again, she said to Molly, "He's actually got people to do everything for him except play basketball. Maybe that's why he even needs someone to say 'I'm sorry' for him."

"I was getting to that, if you'd give me a chance," he said.

"Then get to it," Mattie said.

"I'm sorry," Josh said.

"Really," Molly said.

82

A little too sarcastic. Anytime he was in the area, it was getting to be a reflex with Molly, like when somebody tapped you on your knee.

It was perfect, if you thought about it.

A reflex jerk.

"Really," he said.

He was wearing a knit cap pulled down pretty close to his eyes, maybe to use as some kind of disguise. And he wore his leather jacket. He reached into the inside pocket of it now and pulled out her mom's letter. Somehow he had managed to smooth it out since tossing it in the wastebasket.

"I should have come after you the other night," he said. "And then we had to go to Atlanta over the weekend."

The Celtics had played their second game of the season on the road, Molly knew, beating the Hawks by eight.

"It's easier with you just reading about you in the paper," she said.

"Uh, Mols," Sam said.

Josh seemed to notice him for the first time. "Wait a second," he said. "I know you. You're the kid from the parking lot the other night."

Sam walked over and put out his hand. "Sam Bloom," he said.

Josh shook his hand carefully, Molly thought, as if he still didn't trust him. "Her partner in crime," Josh said.

"We're like the Hardy boys," Sam said. "Except she's not a boy."

Mattie said to Sam, "Son, why don't you and I go set on the front steps and let them talk while I let you talk as much as you want to me."

Before Sam could answer, Mattie took him by the arm and walked him to the front stoop.

"Anyway," Josh said, "Thomas told me where you live, and when I told Mattie the story—"

"You thought you'd stop by."

"You really do sound like her."

"Mattie?"

"Your mom."

Molly put out her hand. "I'd like her letter back, please."

"Not before we talk about it."

"The other day," Molly said, "I had to bribe you with that letter just to get you to talk to me."

He smiled.

"I'll give you the letter back if you give me fifteen minutes," he said.

He was wearing an old gray sweatshirt under the leather jacket, jeans with holes in the knees, work boots. He said they could take a walk. Molly wanted to know how they could do that without people bothering them.

"Sometimes I can walk all around town when I look like this," he said. "The difference between me and other people is that I just can't stop." He nodded at her. "You gonna bring that with you in case we find a hoop?"

Molly had forgotten the basketball under her arm.

She started to go give the ball to Sam, and Josh said, "Nah, bring it. I know this place a couple of blocks away."

"You want me to come with you, in case you start forgetting to act like a human being?" Mattie said from the steps.

"I'm pretty sure I can take it from here," Josh said.

"I may walk down to that Starbucks that looks like the First National Bank of Starbucks," Mattie said. "Call me on my cell when you're ready to go home. I'll meet you back here."

As Molly and Josh started walking toward Mount Vernon Street, Molly looked back at Mattie.

Who just winked at her.

Somehow walking in Beacon Hill with him dressed like he was, stocking cap pulled down tight, looking like a bit of a slob, didn't cause a riot.

There were never a lot of people on the narrow streets once you got up here. Molly had noticed that from the start. It was like a cut-off-from-the-rest-of-the-world world. When there was a lot of traffic noise, you were surprised. Molly could imagine what it was like up here before there were even cars. This was an old part of Boston that hadn't gotten torn down like the old Garden.

They walked in silence for a while, as if neither one of them knew how to start the conversation.

He pointed finally to one of the big old brownstones at the end of Louisburg Square. "I was in that one," he said, "after I signed my first contract. Third year in the league."

She didn't say anything right away. She was trying to figure out why he was different today than the other times, or if he was just different because Mattie was with him.

"What are you doing here?" she said.

Just came out with it. People who didn't know Molly thought she was shy, especially now that she was the new kid in school, something she'd never been before. But most of the time she just acted shy and quiet because she wanted to be left alone.

"You get right to it, don't you?"

"That's not an answer."

He pointed at what looked like a little alley down to their left. Molly had passed it a bunch of times without paying any attention. Collins Walk, the street sign said.

"There's a hoop tucked around a corner at the end of there," he said. "C'mon."

"So why are you here?" Molly said.

"Are you always this tough?"

Molly said, "You would be, too, if you were me."

"Yeah," Josh Cameron said, "I guess I would be."

They walked down Collins Walk and made a right, and there it was, a basket that looked to be the right height to Molly. There was a free-throw line painted in green and the key-shaped lane they had on real courts. It wasn't even a half-court, but there was enough room to shoot around.

"There used to be some kids who lived in this house right here," he said. "I think they moved away. I'm not sure how many people even in the neighborhood know the court's still here."

Molly said, "Listen—"

He put up a hand. "I'm here because I felt rotten about crumpling up the letter and making you cry," he said. "I'm not that bad a guy."

"Could have fooled me."

"I actually came down looking for you, but you weren't on the street when I got out there, and Lindsay the parking guy said he hadn't seen you."

"I went through the hotel. That's when I met Thomas."

"He told me."

"He's nice."

"And I'm not?"

"Not to me," she said.

"Maybe we can start over," he said. "How would that be? You giving me a chance."

"No," Molly said. She slammed the basketball down hard. "You're the one who's got to give me a chance."

"Hold on," he said. "Put yourself in my shoes for a second."

It made Molly smile, no chance of stopping it, as she looked down at his Converse sneakers.

"They're too stinking big."

He said, "You smile like her, too."

He asked for the ball. She bounced it to him. He told her to cut for the hoop. She did. He bounced a ball to her, but it bounced too high. Somehow Molly caught it over her head, brought it down, managed to shoot the ball in the same motion, underhanded, like a little scoop shot.

She didn't think about doing any of it. She just did it. The ball looked like it was off-line when it hit the backboard, but somehow had enough spin on it to go through the net.

When she collected the ball, she noticed him staring at her, a funny look on his face.

He extended his hands again, asking for the ball.

Again without thinking, not even looking at him, Molly casually flipped the ball to him behind her head.

It was just like girls' practice.

The ball just sort of ended up exactly where she wanted it to.

After what seemed like a long time, another long silence, still staring at her, he said, "You're pretty good."

Molly stared back at him.

Neither one of them had noticed that Mattie had followed them to the little court.

"Where in the world do you suppose she gets it from?" Mattie said.

CHAPTER 12

Molly and Sam were sitting on a bench in the Tadpole
Playground, the one with the statue of a frog sitting above the
entrance. Molly liked it there, watching little kids go down the
slides or across the monkey bars, jump down onto a rubbery sur-
face made for soft landings, and mostly just be happy. But usually she had to drag Sam here, because of the frog statues
everywhere you looked.

He'd tell Molly the dopey frogs reminded him too much of
himself, like he was surrounded by all his cousins, and she'd tell
him to shut up.

Which he would.

Until they both had enough of the silence and Sam decided
it was time to tell a joke.

It was another part of their friendship that just was, another
thing that made Molly feel as if she'd known Sam Bloom her
whole life. He was her soft landing.

"I still don't get why he read the letter again after he threw it
away," Sam said now.

"Well, he left out one big part," Molly said. "He did take it out of the wastebasket. That part's true. But Mattie found it on his desk in the morning and read it and started firing questions at him as soon as he got up."

"She reads his mail?" Sam said.

"Like your mom reads your e-mails sometimes," Molly said. "Which sort of figures, because she acts a lot more like his mom than his housekeeper.

"Anyway," Molly said, "Mattie started asking where was I, and he told her what had happened the night before. Then I guess she yelled at him. She told me that she made him read the letter again, but told him to do it with his brain attached to him this time."

This was no Indian summer day in Boston, despite the sun Molly felt on her face. They were lucky, she thought, if the temperature was much more than fifty degrees.

She thought to herself, It would be a beach day in London.

"I may use that," Sam said. "Do something with your brain attached. She's funny."

"So he read it again," Molly said. "And when he did, when he really read it, he decided that nobody except my mom could have written it."

"My butt's cold," Sam said.

"Boy," Molly said, "how did you know that was *exactly* the response I was looking for?"

"It's a gift," he said.

She looked over the pond below them, which nearly stretched all the way to Boylston Street. Once the sun was gone from the sky, it would get dark fast, and they'd both have to go home. It always made Molly sad.

Even knowing she would see Sam the next day at school.

When it was just the two of them this way, before she'd started worrying about the time, when it was just the Frisbee-throwers in the field behind them and the people reading books on all the benches and the dog-walkers and the stroller-walkers all around them, Molly felt . . . normal.

Like a normal kid.

"So as I was saying?" Sam said. "My butt really is cold."

"Is this one of those times when you want me to offer you my jacket to use like a blanket even though you haven't actually asked me to do that?"

"That would be wrong, wrong, wrong," Sam said. "Unless you really are offering."

She had her favorite turtleneck on, one her mom had bought her at Harrod's the previous winter, so she took off her blue down jacket and spread it out for Sam.

"You're telling me that he believes you now?"

Molly said, "Not exactly. He believes her. He told me before he left yesterday that nobody could know that much about the day they broke up, no matter how much they tried to fake it."

"But wouldn't he want to know for sure? About you, I mean?"

"He talked about one of those tests," Molly said. "But I told him I didn't want to do that."

"But you stole his hat," Sam said. "That was a Hardy boy deal if I ever heard one."

"Except I'm a girl," Molly said.

She turned so she was facing Commonwealth Ave. and Two Commonwealth. Looking at his view from this direction today.

Wondering if Josh was up there thinking about her the way she was down here thinking about him.

"I want him to believe me *because* I'm me," she said. "Does that make any sense to you?"

"Hardly any."

"I thought I could use all that DNA stuff to make him come around, but I changed my mind," she said. "I want him to do the thing my mom said he'd never do: Want me for himself."

"You want him to pass the test without you having to give him the answer," Sam said.

"Something like that," Molly said.

"So where do we go from here?"

"He wants to talk to Barbara about this."

Sam stood up, brushing the grass and dirt off her parka before handing it to her.

"You liked him yesterday, didn't you?"

Molly nodded. "Maybe."

Maybe liking him was a start.

She never had any warning when she would miss her mom the most. It could happen when she was sitting in school, or walking across the park, or sitting at the dinner table with Bill and Barbara and Kimmy.

Or sitting alone in her room.

Like now.

Sitting alone and feeling as if she would never get over missing her for as long as she lived.

She did what she always did when she felt like this, and took out her mom's letters.

Read them even though she knew them by heart. Read them and heard her mom's voice inside her head. Saw her face. Heard her laugh. Saw her smile.

Even back when Molly still believed her mom's story about the dad she'd never known, Molly had never felt cheated in the parent department. Not when her mom was still around. If Jen Parker was your mom, you couldn't ever feel cheated about anything. Or feel like you needed anything.

You had her.

"She was always a force of nature," Barbara Evans told Molly once, when she came in and saw Molly reading the letters. "From the first day I knew her."

Once a year at the American School in London, it would be "Bring Dad to School Day." Molly would always bring her mom. And it was all right, with her and her friends and her teachers. Just because everybody loved her mom, always wanted to have her around.

Now her mom was gone, and Molly had no idea where *she* was going, with Josh Cameron especially. After having told herself her whole life that she didn't need a dad, now she wanted one in the worst way. And there he was, right over there on the other side of the park.

The problem was getting over there, for good.

She spread the letters out on the bed, keeping them in order, the way she always did, thinking there might be some great big piece of advice about life she might have missed, something she could use now.

Noticed again how the letters got shorter near the end.

"No matter what," her mom wrote in one of the very last ones, "you know I'll always be with you."

"Let Barb take care of you," another one said. "The way she always wanted to take care of me, except I wouldn't let her."

The last one had the line Molly would use on Barbara the next day when they were walking back across the Public Garden from Two Commonwealth, the one about not being afraid to get hurt.

"I don't want you to be afraid of anything," her mom wrote.

Molly put the letters back into the box when she was done. She read them to make herself feel better, but sometimes they only made her feel worse.

Her homework was finished. There was nothing on TV she wanted to watch. Molly went over to the window and looked out on Joyless Street.

It was a rare evening when Bill Evans came home early from work. And for once he hadn't gone straight to his study after dinner to do more work on his computer or make more business calls. Lately it seemed as if he was on the phone all the time. Molly just assumed it had something to do with another big bank deal.

Tonight was different. Tonight he had even volunteered to take Kimmy and Molly down the hill to Scoop, on Charles Street, for banana splits. Molly loved Scoop's banana splits, but as soon as Bill made the offer, Molly had seen something as clear as day on Kimmy's face: She wanted to have her dad to herself.

"Oh, man, I'd love to," Molly said. "But I've got way too much homework to do. You go, Kimmy. If you think you can make it back up the hill fast enough, bring me one to go. I don't even care if the ice cream has melted a little bit."

Both Bill and Kimmy said that would be fine, they'd walk fast coming home. Kimmy was grinning as though Josh Cameron had just called and asked her to the movies.

Now Molly looked over toward Mount Vernon and saw the two of them walking up the hill toward the brownstone. Bill Evans in his Patriots Windbreaker and jeans and his ancient Reebok shoes. Kimmy next to him in her gray Prescott hoody.

Bill was carrying what had to be Molly's banana split.

Suddenly Kimmy started to laugh. Then she started to run, on those long legs she'd gotten from her father. She ran under a streetlight and Molly could see her face all lit up, like someone had put a spotlight on her. Molly could never remember seeing Kimmy Evans as happy as she looked right now. Maybe because she hardly ever got dad time like this.

Bill was laughing, too, yelling out something that Molly couldn't hear, looking pretty happy himself.

Now he started to jog after his daughter, not running very hard, even though he was trying to act like he wanted to catch her.

Kimmy turned her head and ran faster.

That was when she tripped.

Molly knew what those sidewalks were like. Kimmy'd probably hit one of those raised-up places in the cobblestone that were like a step you weren't expecting.

She went down, hard.

Molly knew Bill Evans's best sport had been football, that he'd been a star halfback at Princeton. Now he ran like one to his daughter, dropping the ice cream bag, sprinting for Kimmy, getting to her in a flash, scooping her up into his arms like he was scooping up a loose ball in a game.

Molly could see Kimmy's chest go up and down as she cried. Saw Bill push the hood back from her face and brush her hair away from her eyes. Saw him use the end of his sleeve to pat away tears.

Then he gently put her down and pulled up one of the legs of the sweatpants Kimmy was wearing, staring at her knee, getting down on his own hands and knees and staring at the knee like he was staring at something through a microscope.

Molly felt like she was spying on them but couldn't make herself turn away.

Then Kimmy was laughing again, as Bill's nose pressed almost to that knee.

They were both laughing.

He scooped her up again, as easily as he would a sack filled with clothes, and walked back to where he'd dropped the ice cream. Kimmy was still laughing, draped over his shoulder.

The only person crying now was Molly.

Even watching from inside the house, watching a real dad with his real daughter, she felt like more of an outsider than ever.

$\mathcal{M}$olly confirmed one of her theories in the first five minutes Barbara was in Josh Cameron's living room.

Barbara hadn't been kidding.

She *really* didn't like him.

She smiled at him the whole time they were talking about the old days, not just talking about Molly's mom but a lot of other people they went to UConn with, some of whose names even Molly recognized. Whatever happened to him? I actually saw her at our tenth year reunion. "No, they got divorced," Barbara said at one point, and Josh said, "Man, I thought he'd gotten life with her without parole." Then they'd laugh.

Except Molly knew Barbara was laughing with every part of her but the place where people meant it when they really laughed: her eyes.

Okay, Molly thought, this isn't what we're looking for.

When they finally ran out of small talk, Mattie appeared with coffee for the grown-ups, a glass of iced tea for Molly. Josh introduced her to Barbara.

After he did, Mattie said, "Was he as big a pain in the butt when he was a college boy as he is now, a sports legend loved by millions?"

It didn't come out as sarcasm with Mattie, just pure fun.

"Worse," Barbara said, not quite so playfully.

"Figured," Mattie said. To Josh she said, "If they ask you any real hard questions, I'll just be in the kitchen."

When she was gone it was as if somebody had suddenly shut off the volume in the room.

"So," Josh said to Barbara.

"So," Barbara said.

Over her shoulder, Molly could see the kitchen door push open a crack.

"Listen, Barb," Josh said, "I always thought I could trust you."

"Always," she said.

Now *that* was sarcasm, Molly thought.

If Josh noticed, he just ignored it. "So," he said again, "I'm going to trust you now."

"Molly was very mysterious about why you needed to see me," she said.

Josh said, "I asked her. And I'm going to ask you to keep what I'm about to tell you between the three of us. And your husband, of course. It's important."

"I'm sure Molly's told you I have a daughter. Kimmy. The same age as Molly."

"Probably like sisters," Josh said, with a quick glance toward Molly.

"You bet!" Molly said.

Another gag job, but it got a real smile out of Barbara, the first one since she'd walked through the front door.

"I can't imagine you could tell me anything that I couldn't tell my daughter," she said.

"You might not want to make a decision on that until you hear what I need to tell you," he said.

Molly was expecting a scene, but Barbara shocked her. Mostly by not being shocked.

"I never believed the story about that guy loving her and leaving her over there," she said, almost to herself, like she was alone in the room. "That wasn't her style, for one thing."

To Josh she said, "I should have guessed that you were always going to be the only one for her, no matter how much she tried to deny it." She nodded. "Even if she was the one who broke it off."

She looked at Molly, then at Josh, then back at Molly.

"If you really think about it, it all makes perfect sense, Molly being yours," she said.

"*If* she is mine," Josh said, a little too quickly. "I'm not saying it's for sure yet."

Molly let that go for now.

Barbara said, "I'm not sure I understand you."

"All I'm saying," Josh said, "is that my first reaction was that it was just a made-up story from a kid . . . from Molly, because she wanted it to be true. Or maybe it was some kind of shakedown."

That got Molly's attention. "Shakedown?"

"For money," he said. "It's never happened to me. But it's happened to other guys in sports I know or I've heard about. A woman they used to know shows up with a kid they say is his.

Sometimes the guy pays off without even having one of those tests, just to make the whole thing go away. They'll cut a deal."

"Even if it really is the guy's own child?" Molly said.

"Let me explain something to you about athletes, especially ones making a ton of money when they never thought they'd have any money in their lives," he said. "They'll do anything to keep somebody else from getting their hands on it. And sometimes," he said, "they just don't want to know what they don't want to know."

Molly was almost positive she could hear Mattie make some kind of snorting noise from the other side of the kitchen door.

"Mom would have never done that," Molly said.

"For one thing," Barbara said, "she was physically incapable of telling a lie." Barbara sighed one of her big Barb sighs, a sound that always made Molly think it had come out of a musical instrument. "Even though I would tell her one wouldn't hurt occasionally, after she had delivered another one of her famous honest opinions about me."

"Brutally honest," Josh said. "Oh, that was Jen, all right."

"The only person she ever lied to was herself," Barbara said.

"About what?"

"About you."

"I don't understand."

"No surprise there," Barbara said.

This wasn't good.

"Where we goin' with this?" Josh said. "What do you mean she lied to herself about me?"

"About how much you hurt her," Barbara said.

Molly felt as uncomfortable as on her first day at the Prescott

School, when she didn't know anybody and didn't want to, wanted to be anywhere except in what was called a home room and felt like anything but.

She finally said, "Does anybody mind if I change the subject for a second?"

"Be my guest," Josh said.

Molly said, "I thought you believed us now. Mom and me."

"I believe *she* believed you're . . . ours," he said. "And I know you believe it."

"But you don't?"

Josh said, "The simplest way would be for us to take one of those tests, that way—"

"No!" Molly couldn't help it, it came out of her as a shout.

They both looked at her. Molly could see Mattie's face in the door.

Molly shook her head. "No, no, no," she said. "You have to believe me because you believe me."

"I'm just saying—"

"I know what you're just saying," Molly said. "My mom didn't lie, and I don't lie. And if you still think I'm lying, then I guess we're all wasting our time here."

"It's not what I meant," Josh said.

"I don't want your stupid money," she said, "if that's all you're worried about."

Now nobody said anything, until Mattie suddenly burst through the doors, saying, "What he's trying to say is that he wants to get to know you." She gave Josh Cameron a good whack on the shoulder. "Isn't that right, Mr. Words?"

"I was getting to that."

"He wants a different kind of test, he just doesn't know how to ask for it," Mattie said. "A test where you get to know him and he gets to know you. Then we can cross all those other bridges and so forth when we come to them."

Molly imagined that it was like some cartoon comet had crashed into the room. Mattie, as little as she was, had done everything but trail a flame behind her.

"But we can't get there," Mattie said, "without Mrs. Evans's permission." One more whack on the shoulder for Josh. "Isn't that right?"

"That's one of the reasons I wanted to talk to you," Josh said. "It's not like she can just start spending time with Mattie and me without your say-so, Barb. She is in your custody, after all."

"Yes, she is," Barbara said pointedly.

"You've got to let me," Molly said.

"No, actually, I don't."

"But it's what Mom wanted," Molly said.

Another whopper of a lie, one Barbara saw right through. "Somehow I doubt that," she said. "Now who's not being honest here?"

"She wanted me to get to know my father."

"Well, she sure took her time getting *there.*"

"Please," Molly said. She knew it sounded like begging, didn't care.

"Say I do go along," Barbara said. "What are we supposed to tell people? What am I supposed to tell Kimmy?"

She was talking to Josh, but Mattie answered.

"How about the truth?" Mattie said. "I've been over there on the other side of the door, listening to you all talk about the truth."

"Eavesdropping, it's called," Josh said.

She made a motion like she was swatting away a fly.

"Just tell people the truth," Mattie said. "That this little angel here is the daughter of a college friend who died. Who doesn't have any parents now and just came back to America. And how you didn't know the mom had died, but now you do, and how you met the angel and took a shine to her."

Barbara said, "My daughter's not stupid. Neither is my husband."

"So they must have a pretty good sense of what this little girl is all about by now," Mattie said. "Just tell them that Josh Cameron is a sucker for a story like this." She gave him a look. "The way most normal people would be."

Josh looked at Barbara. "This hasn't been an easy thing for me to find out," Josh said. "Now I need to figure out the best way for me to handle it."

Barbara Evans stood up.

"Well, it's nice to see one thing hasn't changed," she said. "It's still all about you."

CHAPTER 14

*Y*ou knew all along," Molly said when they were outside. "Didn't you?"

"I knew the minute I set eyes on you at the airport," Barbara said. "It was like looking at Josh. The young Josh, anyway."

"Did you ever say anything to Mom?"

"Your mom and I always had the same arrangement, from when we ended up roommates freshman year," Barbara said. "If she wanted me to know something, she told me. I have a feeling it worked that way with him, too. If she'd wanted him to know about you, she would have told him."

They were cutting across the Public Garden, past the big statue of George Washington that just said "Washington" on it, as if asking everybody, Is there another Washington worth talking about?

"This is a bad idea, Molly," Barbara said. "A monumentally bad idea."

"How come you didn't say that back there?"

"I told him I'd think about it," Barbara said. "Now I have."

"For ten minutes?" Molly said.

"I could have given him an answer in ten seconds," Barbara said. "Your mother was the smart one to the end, obviously. He wasn't good enough for her, and he isn't good enough for you."

"I'm afraid that's not your decision to make."

"I'm afraid it is."

Molly stopped near Washington.

"No," she said.

She'd been saying that a lot today.

"Molly—"

"You're not *not* letting me do this."

Barbara motioned for them to sit down at the long bench with the tiny statues of ducklings marching along the path in front of them. Molly liked the ducklings as much as she liked old Washington.

And she loved this park. Though not so much right now, with Barbara.

"Hear me out," Barbara said. "There's more to this than you know."

"No," Molly said, "you hear me out."

"This doesn't even sound like you."

Molly said, "Why? Because I don't sound like the good orphan girl everybody wants me to be?"

"He won't be the father you want him to be. He can't."

"But he *is* my father," Molly said. "He's the only real family I have in the whole world."

"He's Josh Cameron," Barbara said. "Who frankly hasn't changed much since college, except that he's a lot richer now." She reached over and took Molly's hands before Molly had a chance to stick them somewhere. "Do you really and truly believe he's going to make room for a child in his life? You think he won't hurt you? Nobody ever hurt your mom the way he did."

"I'm not a child," Molly said.

"Really."

"Next year I'm a teenager," she said. She took her hands away so she could brush imaginary hair off her forehead. "And I already feel older than everybody in my class except Sam."

"You know what I'm saying."

"No, I really don't," Molly said.

A Frisbee landed at their feet. Molly looked up to see that a girl about her age was coming for it. In the distance, she could see the man who was probably the girl's father, yelling, "Sorry."

Molly stood up, made a perfect throw back to him, and sat down.

"You're going to get your heart broken," Barbara said.

Molly shook her head, hard. "If my heart hasn't been broken already, it's not going to get broken."

"I meant more broken," Barbara said. She stopped now and made a sound that was about halfway to a scream, causing a couple who'd just walked past them turn to see what the problem was. "God, there is just too much going on right now."

Molly said, "You okay?"

Barbara smiled. "Not exactly."

"You said before there were things I didn't know," Molly said. "You didn't mean just me and Josh, did you?"

"Something's come up in the last week with Bill's job."

Molly waited.

"I was going to tell you last night, you and Kimmy at the same time. But then you told me we had to go see Josh today, it

106

was important . . ." She clapped her hands together. "Out with it, Barbara."

"Out with what?"

"We're moving," Barbara said.

"Moving," Molly said.

"At the end of the year."

"Where?" Molly asked.

"Los Angeles."

She might as well have said the moon.

Bill's bank had originally wanted someone from Tokyo to open the office in Los Angeles, but that man had left the company suddenly. It was a big promotion for Bill, but the timetable had stayed the same.

"That's what all the phone calls late at night have been about," Molly said.

"It's a huge moment in his career," Barbara said, "and they promise it will only be a few years, tops. But he has to be there by the first of the year, and we've made the decision that we don't want to be separated."

"So you're going."

"Right after Christmas," Barbara said. "We're all going."

"No!" Molly said. "Not now. You can't. *I* can't."

"It's another reason why the whole you-and-Josh thing is a bad idea," Barbara said. "I can't let you start something neither one of you can finish."

"But he's my father," Molly said, knowing she was repeating herself, not caring.

"Molly," Barbara said, trying to make her voice as gentle as possible. "You can't possibly think that you are going to live happily ever after as daddy's little girl."

"But . . . if I leave now, I'll never even find out what could have happened."

"Which might be a good thing."

"You have to let me at least try," Molly said. All-in now, she thought, like one of Sam's poker shows. "I'm not saying I'm going to live happily ever after, or whatever," she said. "But you've got to at least give me the chance to get to know him before we go. *Please*, Barbara."

"I don't want him to hurt you the way he hurt your mother."

"You keep saying that."

"Only because I mean it."

So Molly hit her with the line from her mom.

"My mom always said that if you were afraid to get hurt, you were afraid to be really alive," Molly said.

Barbara stared at her a long time and then said, in an even quieter voice than before, "Still the smart one."

They had the family meeting about Los Angeles at dinner. Kimmy didn't even act surprised. Then when her dad pressed her a little, she admitted she might have been listening outside his study door one night when she came to say good night to him, so she'd had a couple of days to think about it.

Even more surprising was Kimmy's excitement about going.

"Boston's all you've ever known, honey," Barb said.

"Knowing and loving are two different things," Kimmy said.

Tell me about it, Molly thought.

"First of all, I hate the Prescott School for Snobs," Kimmy

said. "And, like, are you kidding? Who wouldn't want to go to Hollywood? I am going to be soooooo *OC*."

"You watch that show?" Bill Evans said. "You're twelve."

"Dad, get real," Kimmy said.

"Yeah, Dad," Barb said, putting her hand on his. "Get real."

Molly sat there and watched them building excitement about the move, talking about where they might live. Barb told Kimmy and Molly about two schools she'd checked out for them, both willing to accept them at midyear. Molly remembered how different it was when her mom told her they were going to Boston, trying to make it sound this exciting for Molly, even though both of them knew they were going because this was her mom's last chance.

"You're sure you're okay with this, Molly?" Bill Evans said. "You were just getting used to Boston."

Molly decided the best thing to do was fake it.

"If Kimmy's ready to go Hollywood," she said, "so am I."

"Wow," Bill said, "I thought this would be harder. We really are good to go then."

She wasn't going, of course. She wasn't leaving Boston, and she wasn't leaving Josh, and she wasn't moving to the other side of the country.

But there was no reason why they had to know that.

"You're *moving*?" Sam said, the words coming out more like a groan.

"*They're* moving," Molly said. "Not me."

"Do they know that?"

"Right."

"Don't worry, you can live with us," Sam said. "I'll fix it with my mom."

"I'm not going to have to," Molly said, then she told him about going to Josh's apartment and how Barbara had finally agreed afterward to let Molly and Josh take things in baby steps in the little time they had left in Boston. Sam asked what baby steps meant, exactly, and Molly told him.

She could go to home games as long as they weren't on school nights. She could go to Saturday afternoon games; Barbara had checked the schedule and noticed that the Celtics had a handful of them early in the season. If there was a late practice and Josh said it was all right for Molly to attend, Mattie could pick her up after school and drive her up to Waltham, on the condition that she finish her homework first, during study hall.

And if anybody asked about this sudden friendship between Josh Cameron and young Molly Parker, they were to all stick to the script that Mattie had pretty much laid out for them in Josh's apartment: Josh Cameron had developed a soft spot for the daughter of an old school friend, one who'd come up with all these colorful ways to finally meet him.

"It's like *Annie*," Sam said. "Except that Daddy Warbucks plays point guard for the Celtics."

"And he isn't bald," Molly said. "And I don't have the cute dog."

"Would it kill you to work with me once in a while?"

"And I don't have curly hair," Molly said. "And I can't carry a tune to save my life—"

110

"You know what's sad?" Sam said. "People think you're the quiet one." There was a pause, and Sam said, "Are you going to tell Josh?"

"Tell him what?"

"That you're moving."

"I'm not moving."

"You know what I'm saying."

"No," Molly said. "I told Barbara not to say anything. I'm not even telling Mattie."

"The thinking on this being?"

"I know Josh Cameron is famous for playing under pressure," Molly said. "But he's already under enough pressure from me."

There was another pause, and then Sam said, "You think you can do this?"

"What?"

"Win him over in six weeks."

"Let me ask you something," Molly said. "Do I have a choice?"

CHAPTER 15

They were waiting for Mattie to come pick them up and take them to the Celtics-Knicks game that night at the new Garden. A Friday night game. After the game, they'd all stop for pizza and then Josh would bring them home. When Molly had asked if Sam could come along, Josh had said, "Tell the partner in crime he's always welcome."

Sam wanted to know if "partner in crime" was going to be permanent, and Molly said it was better than the other nickname Josh had for him, which was "Sam the bad actor."

For some reason, Molly expected Mattie to be driving. Instead, she showed up in a shiny black Town Car. When she got out of the backseat, Molly saw she was wearing the same coat as before, the same black beret.

She gestured to the car and said, "Welcome to his world. If it wasn't for him having to play the games, I worry the boy's feet would never touch the floor."

"Is Josh already at the Garden?" Molly said.

"Drove himself over there a little while ago," she said. "Him and his agent. Least *he* calls him an agent."

Sam said, "What do you call him, Mattie?"

"The squirrel getting four percent," she said.

"I take it you don't like him very much," Molly said.

"You'll probably meet him tonight," Mattie said. "Check out his eyes while he's talking to you. They're always looking every which way, in case somebody drops a twenty-dollar bill and he has to pounce on it."

"Are you insane?" Bobby Fishman was saying.

"You're shouting at me again," Josh said.

"Not at you," Bobby said. "I am just shouting in general. General managers I shout at. Owners I shout at. Sportswriters? I live to shout at them. But shout at a client? Never. On my mother's grave."

"Your mother lives in Boca Raton and plays golf four days a week," Josh said.

"It's an expression," Bobby said.

"You called me insane."

"Only because you are."

Bobby Fishman was in the passenger seat of the Navigator, holding his BlackBerry in his hand as if it were a grenade he thought might go off at any second.

"I'm not insane," Josh said.

"Crazy people never think they are."

"I can't be nice to this kid?"

"Nice is sending her an autographed picture and tickets to the game," Bobby said. "You want to be nice? Buy her a pony. But please don't start bringing a kid around, one who may or may not be your daughter. You think the press might find a story like that interesting? Because I sort of do."

He looked out his window. "Where are we, by the way? Providence?"

"Don't worry about it," Josh said.

"You're absolutely right," Bobby said. "I have enough to worry about with Little Miss Marker."

"Who?"

"Never mind, you're too young," Bobby said.

"Her name is Molly."

"Before you do another thing with her, you and Little Miss Molly are taking one of those tests."

"We can't."

"Hello?" Bobby said into his BlackBerry now, like it was a microphone. "Earth to Josh. Of course you can take one of those tests. You go to the hospital, they take a little blood or hair or saliva or whatever they do, and then we eliminate the guess-work."

"We can't," Josh said. "At least not yet."

"And this is because?"

"Because Molly doesn't want us to."

"Oh," Bobby said, "of course, that explains everything. I mean, why wouldn't we want the twelve-year-old to call the shots here?"

"She wants me to believe her on my own," Josh said.

"Just to be sporting, let me ask you a question," Bobby said. "*Do* you believe her?"

Josh was surprised at how easily the word came out of him. Like he was on the court. Not thinking. Just reacting.

"No," he said to Bobby Fishman.

"No?"

Josh said, "I don't believe Jen—that's her mom, the one who died—would have kept this from me all these years. And when she found out she was dying, I can't believe she thought I was that much of a loser that she couldn't even tell me then."

"I could have told her," Bobby said. "You don't even lose at cards."

"I mean a loser as a guy," Josh said. "As a person. The guy she was in love with once, even if she's the one who dumped me."

"*She* dumped *you*?"

Josh Cameron turned the radio back on. Loud. "Long story," he said. "And you know how you hate long stories."

"So let me get this straight," Bobby Fishman said. He was happy now. He could talk in his normal loud voice, above the music. "You don't believe her, but you're going to hang around with her anyway?"

"She's a nice kid," he said, "for a kid."

"Whether she's yours or not."

"Whether she's mine or not," Josh Cameron said. "I'd only say this to you. But even if she is mine, I've got no place for her in my life."

"But you're going to keep her around until . . . ?" Bobby Fishman let his voice disappear through his open window.

"Until," Josh said, "I can find a nice way to get rid of her."

Bobby Fishman smiled.

"I love it when you think like a big-time sports agent," he said.

CHAPTER 16

Kimmy hardly ever took the same bus home that Molly and Sam did, because of ballet. But she was with them today because her ballet teacher, the one trying to make the Prescott School version of *The Nutcracker* look at least something like the real one, had called in sick.

Now she was trying to act excited that Molly and Sam were getting to go up to Waltham for the Celtics practice.

"There's something I'm not getting," Kimmy said.

"Out of the many, many things you don't get?" Sam said from the seat behind her.

He couldn't help himself when Kimmy was around.

"Wasn't talking to you," she said.

"Just making an observation," Sam said.

"If you say mean things to me, I'll say them back to you," Kimmy said.

"I'm pretty sure you've run out of things to say about the way I look," Sam said. "I just look at it as somebody shooting spitballs at a battleship."

"Well," Kimmy said, "you *are* as wide as Old Ironsides—"

Sam grabbed his chest with both hands, as if he'd been shot. "Oh no," he said, looking down in fake horror, "I'm hit."

"I was trying to have a conversation with Molly," Kimmy said.

"Okay," Molly said. "What don't you get?"

"I don't get how, in a couple of weeks, you've gone from nowhere to being his best friend."

She didn't even have to say who she was talking about. By now Kimmy was obsessed with Josh and his relationship with Molly.

"I guess he just feels sorry for me," Molly said. "I'm sure he'll get tired of having me around. Look how fast *you* got tired of having me around."

The bus pulled up at the bottom of Mount Vernon Street. They all got out.

"You know I'm not tired of having you around," Kimmy said. "And, besides, we're not talking about me. We're talking about Josh Cameron."

"All Josh," Sam said, "all the time."

Kimmy ignored him.

"This is like one of those music videos," she said. "Like the one my mom made me watch one time on MTV. The one where Bruce Springsteen picked out the girl from *Friends* to dance with him on the stage."

"Courteney Cox," Sam said. " 'Dancing in the Dark.' "

Kimmy stared at him. Molly said, "Don't even ask why he knows. He just knows everything."

Kimmy walked ahead of them up the hill.

"One of these days," she said over her shoulder, "I will, too."

Just loud enough for Molly to hear, Sam Bloom said, "There's something to live for."

Mattie drove Molly and Sam up to the Sports Authority Training Center, walked them through the lobby and into the gym, and said that she had some shopping to do and Josh would drive them back to the city.

"He doesn't mind?" Molly said.

"Not after I told him he didn't mind," Mattie said, and left.

As soon as L. J. Brown, who'd pretty much adopted Molly from the first day she showed up at practice, spotted her walking into the gym, he called out, "Well, if it isn't Miss Miss."

The Celtics had just stopped scrimmaging and were taking a water break.

Molly, wearing the Celtics cap L.J. had given her turned backward on her head, came right back at him, because she knew that's what he expected her to do.

"Should a thirty-nine-percent shooter really be using the word *miss* twice in the same sentence?" she said as he reached down to give her a high-five.

L.J. laughed his high-pitched laugh, the one that made him sound like he was wheezing. Then he made a shooting motion with his right hand. "Miss Miss," he said, "from downtown."

The Celtics coach, Paul Gubbins, came over and gave a little pull on the bill of Molly's cap. "Stop distracting my players," he said. "You know how easy that is."

"Hey, Coach," Molly said.

"Hey, kiddo."

118

Molly knew already that no matter what was happening with the Celtics, in a game or at practice, Coach Gubbins was the calmest one of all of them, somehow in control of everything without ever raising his voice or blowing a whistle. Josh said one time over pizza that the only time Paul Gubbins ever stood up during a game was if a couple of players were blocking his view.

He was another one who had been nice to Molly from her first day at practice. Now he called her his assistant coach in charge of "quality control." When he gave her the title, she said, "Wouldn't the head coach be in charge of quality control?"

"Only when they let me," he'd said.

"When they let you?"

"Molly," he said, "there's a reason why I've lasted as long as I have, and the reason is that I figured out a long time ago that these guys *allow* me to coach them."

When the water break was over, the Celtics went back to allowing him to coach them, and Sam and Molly took their usual places, sitting on one of the basket supports. As usual, Josh was so focused on basketball that he didn't even seem to notice them.

That was all right with Molly. She was as thrilled watching them practice up close this way as she was watching games from Josh's seats behind the Celtics bench. And it wasn't just watching Josh. It was L.J. and Nick Tutts and Terry Thompson—the size of them and the way they could move, at least when the bigger guys weren't pounding on each other under the basket. It was their grace, the way they could make basketball look almost beautiful.

This was ballet, she thought.

Coach Gubbins sat with his legs crossed and watched while Josh played the role of coach on the floor. The slaps and grunts and squeak of the new sneakers in the echoing gym were like music.

And for the first time since her mom had died, Molly felt like she was a part of something. Like some big, crazy family. She didn't feel like that with the Evanses and knew she probably never would. She didn't feel that way at school, or even when she was visiting the Blooms, as much as Mrs. Bloom tried to make Molly feel at home.

She certainly wasn't close to feeling that way at Josh's, even with Mattie around.

Yet somehow she felt that way at Celtics practice, even with the players who acted embarrassed because Molly had to keep reminding them what her name was.

She didn't know where all this was going, mostly because she didn't know where things with Josh and her were going.

What she knew was this: She sure liked being a Boston Celtic.

As soon as practice was over, L.J. grabbed her hand and pulled her off the basket support.

"Okay, Miss Miss," he said, "let's see how much game you brought here with you today."

"Can Sam play, too?" she said.

"No, no, no," Sam said. "You guys go ahead. I wouldn't want to show you up."

Molly could swear Sam was starting to sweat, even thinking about playing a little ball with her and L.J.

"You're sure?" she said.

"I'll just sit here and think deep thoughts," he said.

"Can't you do both?" L.J. said, joking with him.

"Of course I *can*," Sam said. "I just don't choose to."

Sometimes Molly wasn't sure how much Sam really loved sports, even with all the sports information he had inside his amazing head. But he knew how much Molly loved coming to practice, how much she missed it when the Celtics went out of town for a couple of days. So he came with her when he could.

Sam being Sam.

Molly dribbled around a little bit, even put the ball behind her back because she knew that would get a rise out of L.J.

He whistled and said, "You know what they say?"

"What do they say?"

"You go, girl."

Molly drove to the basket and laid the ball in. When she dribbled back up to the top of the key, L.J. came over to guard her, even if they both knew he was just out there as a kind of prop to make her look good. And feel good. So Molly gave him a little head fake. L.J. let her get a step on him. When she got inside, not even knowing what she was doing, she leaned her left shoulder into him, catching him in his hip, stepped back, and made what passed for her jump shot, even though she didn't jump, mostly just got the ball on her right shoulder and shoved it toward the basket.

"Well, now, look at Miss Miss and her moves," he said, "creating space for herself and everything. Just like Josh Cameron, star of stars."

Molly looked over to see if Josh had seen her shot. Or was even paying attention to her and L.J. But his back was to her. The

Celtics had a policy that the writers and TV people and radio people couldn't come into the gym until practice was over. So they had filed in now, like kids on a fire drill. As usual, they had gone right to Josh, surrounding him to the point where Molly could only see the back of his head in the center of the television lights that seemed to follow him everywhere.

"Okay," L.J. said, "we got time for a quick game of H-O-R-S-E."

Molly looked at him with her serious face.

"Am I allowed to dunk?" she said.

L.J. gave her his *he-he-he* laugh and told her she could have first shot and the rules were the same as always. No dunking from him, no left-handed shots, no going so far outside she couldn't reach the basket.

And he had to try.

After about fifteen minutes, during which Molly felt like she couldn't miss any of the simple shots she was taking, the game was even at H-O-R-S to H-O-R-S. Some of the Celtics players, the ones who had been doing some extra shooting at the other end of the court, came down to watch.

Nick Tutts said, "Um, L.J.?"

"What up?"

"If you lose, it will only be a secret between all of us and everybody at Molly's school. Isn't that right, Molly?"

Molly nodded.

"That ain't right," L.J. said. "You know the deal, right, Miss Miss?"

"No deals at game point," Molly said, and the rest of the Celtics hooted.

L.J. pointed a finger at her and said, "What happens in Waltham stays in Waltham."

Molly flipped him the ball. "Your shot, big fella."

L.J. missed a turnaround jumper in the lane. Molly went to the free-throw line, which was about as far away from the basket as she could get, and threw her longest shot at the basket.

Swish.

Now the Celtics sitting on the floor at half-court stomped their feet and clapped and whistled.

L.J. missed.

But because it was game point, he got to shoot again. Molly passed him the ball. He went through his whole foul-shooting routine, bounced the ball a couple of times.

Made it.

Game still on.

Now Molly decided to try a shot she'd been practicing, mostly because it was one of Josh's signature shots, one he said he'd copied from Bob Cousy, who he told sportswriters would always be the greatest Celtics point guard of them all. It was a shot he could only shoot when he was open. The motion for it always made Molly think of somebody pushing a friend over a fence. Josh would stop short of whoever was guarding him, and his left knee would go up in the air at the same time the ball did in his right hand.

His right foot would never leave the ground.

Molly tried to do it exactly that way now.

Made it.

More cheers from the Celtics.

"Aw, man, I hate that dinky old-school stuff," L.J. said.

And missed.

Then he missed again.

Ball game.

L.J. laid down on his back, kicked his legs wildly in the air, then went completely still. "Take me now, Lord," he said. "I done lost to a girl."

"Hey, watch it there," Molly said.

She looked over again to where Josh was with the reporters. He still had his back turned. Even the commotion L.J. was causing, making the end of practice sound more like recess, didn't get him to turn around.

Molly went back and sat with Sam until Josh was finished answering the reporters' questions.

When he finally came over, he said, "You guys have fun?"

Molly almost said, Like you care.

But didn't.

"It was great," Molly said.

Josh said, "What was going on with L.J. when he was making so much noise? I could barely hear the questions those guys were asking, even if they were the same ones they ask me every day."

Molly tried to tell him about the H-O-R-S-E game as fast as she could, but knew as soon as she started that it was like trying to tell somebody about some neat TV show they'd missed, or some movie.

"Great," Josh said, with about as much enthusiasm as if she'd told him she'd just bought a new backpack for school.

Just as they were about to walk out the side door of the gym, the one that led to the parking lot, Adam Burke walked through the same door, out of breath, looking more like a college kid than ever, Molly thought. This one late for class.

"Hey, man, I got stuck in traffic. I was afraid I was going to miss you," he said to Josh.

Josh grinned. "I'll give you my answers bumper-sticker style," he said. "We might be better than last year. Young guys fitting in faster than I thought they would."

"But it's still early," Adam said.

"And," Josh said, pointing a finger at him, "it's a long season."

"Really long," Adam said.

It was then that he noticed Molly and Sam.

"Hey," Uncle Adam of the *Boston Globe* said. "What are you guys doing here?"

CHAPTER 17

$\mathcal{M}$olly looked at Sam. Sam looked at her. Then they both looked at Josh.

"Forget about that," Josh said to Adam Burke. "Where you been at, man? Have I seen you since opening night?"

Adam said he had never gotten to take any time off after the World Series, so after the Celtics' opener he'd gone to Los Angeles for a couple of weeks to stare at movie stars drinking cappuccino and try to pitch movie ideas.

"Got any good ones?" Josh said.

"Not according to any of the producers I talked to," he said. "All of whom looked to be about Sam and Molly's age." He nodded at them. "So what are they doing at practice?"

"Not for print?" Josh said.

It was interesting, Molly noticed. He wasn't talking to Adam like he was Sam's uncle. He was talking to him like he was a sportswriter. And maybe a snoopy one at that.

"Aw, don't do that to me on a day when I got here late," Adam said, almost whining. " 'Not for print' always means it's something good."

"Not for print?" Josh said again.

"Fine."

Josh said, "Sam must've told you about Molly's mom. Did he mention that we went to college together? Her mom and me?"

"He might have."

"After a few minutes with me," Sam said, "what he mostly hears is *blah blah blah*." Sam tried to raise his eyebrows but failed miserably, as usual. "Even when I'm telling him an interesting story."

"Shut up, junior," Adam said.

"Shutting up," Sam said.

"Anyway," Josh said, "now that I've gotten to know Molly a little, I decided that maybe she could use another friend."

Molly watched him as he said that and noticed something she'd noticed before: When he was playing the part of Good-Guy Josh, when he wanted somebody to like him, he had this way of putting his hand in his hair and mussing it all up, the way a kid would.

Totally phony.

"Pretty cool," Adam Burke said.

"I'm just doing what anybody would do."

Now Josh tried to put his arm around Molly. She knew it was just for show. She pulled away, bent down, untied her shoelaces so she could make herself real busy tying them back up.

One of these days, he was going to put his arm around her— hug her, even—and mean it.

"Aw, man, this is a perfect column for me," Adam Burke said.

"Not happening."

"And did I mention that it's a slow news day?"

"Write about what a long season it is," Josh said, grinning. "Your readers need to know stuff like that."

"Very funny."

"I'm not doing this because I want publicity," Josh said.

Sam had moved behind Josh and Adam. Molly saw him stick a finger in his throat. Gag me.

"I'm doing it," Josh continued, "because this girl has gone through a lot and came through it as a greater kid than ever."

Sam must have put his finger too far into his throat, because he actually started coughing now. Josh and Adam turned around. Sam put up a hand, as if indicating that nobody was going to have to do the Heimlich maneuver on him.

"I can write the living . . . daylights out of this," Adam said.

"I'm sure you could," Josh said.

"Think about it, at least?" Adam said.

"Okay, I'll think about it," Josh said to him.

To Molly and Sam he said, "C'mon, you guys, we gotta bounce."

"You, Josh Cameron, are their ride home?" Adam said.

"Pretty much."

"Aw, man, you're killing me."

Josh tried to put his arm around Molly one more time as they walked out the door into the parking lot. She pulled away again, saying "don't" as she ran ahead of him.

"God, you're tough," he said.

"Runs in the family," Molly said.

By now Molly had discovered that there were two floors to Josh Cameron's condominium at Two Commonwealth. The first floor was all him. Upstairs was Mattie's room, her small kitchen, a laundry room, and a spare bedroom that Mattie used for television watching.

That one had become Molly's when Barbara would allow her to stay over once in a while after a Friday home game and a late pizza at Upper Crust.

When Josh finally woke up—he could sleep, Molly had decided, even better than he could play basketball—Mattie would whip them up some pancakes and for a little while, it would feel like a regular Saturday morning for Molly.

With a regular dad.

Even though there was nothing regular about this situation at all.

And she was running out of time to make it regular.

Sometimes she felt as if she were putting a gigantic puzzle together a piece or two at a time, first one corner and then the other. Knowing as she did that it wasn't coming together nearly as fast as she wanted it to.

Or needed it to.

And sometimes she wondered if she could ever make the pieces fit the way she wanted them to.

He didn't know how to talk to her, for one thing. Didn't know how to *be* with her. It's why, Molly was sure, he always had Mattie around when Molly came to visit, why he had Mattie bring Molly to practices and games. When he didn't know how to talk to her, Mattie could do the talking. And when Mattie wasn't around, if she was having dinner with friends or having a night off, that was when Josh struggled. They'd rent a movie, and he'd start watching it with her. But then he'd seem almost relieved when his cell phone would go off—instead of a ring or a chirp, it played "Beast of Burden" by the Rolling Stones—and he'd have to leave the room to go talk to somebody. And wouldn't come back for what would feel like half an hour.

Then Mattie would be back, and Molly would want to laugh, hearing Josh telling her how the two of them had watched a movie together. Only it wasn't like that, not at all.

Molly noticed the only time he was with other people, *really* with them, was when he was playing basketball with his teammates, and Molly didn't count that. That was basketball. The rest of the time, he seemed happiest when he was alone, even the kind of alone he had going for him when he was with somebody.

It was weird, Molly had decided. Here was somebody the whole world thought of as the best team guy going, the one everybody else held up, even from other sports, as the ultimate team player.

But as soon as the game was over, all he wanted to do was be by himself. It's why Molly wondered if her mom had been right about him, that Josh Cameron couldn't really *be* with anybody. That all he needed to be happy was himself.

Molly was going to New York with the Celtics.

She had spent the night in the guest room after the Celtics had won their Friday night game against the Washington Wizards. The plan from there was for Josh to go to a late-morning practice in Waltham, leave with the team for the airport, where the team's own plane was waiting for them. Molly and Mattie would take the shuttle down to New York about the same time.

When Josh finally got up about ten, Mattie fixed them all pancakes. He said that since they were all going to get to New York about the same time, anyway, he'd have a car waiting for them at LaGuardia to take them to the team's hotel. Then they could all go out to an early dinner somewhere, or just have room service. He said the hotel, the Sherry-Netherland, had what he described as some la-di-da restaurant right off its lobby.

"Sounds like a plan, right?" Josh said.

Mattie said to Molly, "That okay with you, hon?"

"That's what I was asking Molly," Josh said.

Mattie winked. "We're just doing what us girls do all the time," she said. "Eliminating the middleman."

Molly said to both of them, "The shuttle with Mattie sounds like fun. I've never been to New York in my whole life."

Mattie said, "Done deal, then."

She put out her hand for Molly to give her five.

"Road trip," Mattie said.

After breakfast, Mattie walked her back to 1A Joyless Street. Molly picked out some clean clothes, packed them in her duffel, then called Sam to tell him about the road trip.

"Cool," he said. Then he asked how much money she was bringing with her. "No money," Molly said. Sam said, "What?" and told her she sounded like a rookie, that you couldn't go on the road without what he called "mad money." Then he told her that he'd meet her in front of Two Commonwealth in fifteen minutes and explain.

He was waiting at the corner of Commonwealth and Arlington when Molly and Mattie got back.

"Here," he said, handing Molly a wadded-up roll of bills that he said added up to a hundred and twenty dollars. Out of what he called his "emergency fund."

"Now are you going to tell me what mad money is?" Molly said.

Sam said, "My mom said that when she was single, she always took money with her when she'd go out on a date, in case she got mad and wanted to go home."

"I don't need this," Molly said. "I sort of don't see that happening in New York."

"You never know," Sam said.

Molly said, "I'm going to think of it as glad money."

"Glad?"

"Glad to be going," she said. "Maybe I'll buy you a present with your own money."

"Wouldn't that be like me buying myself a present?"

Molly gave him a quick hug, which she knew always embarrassed him, and said, "It's the thought that counts," and then told him she'd give him a full report on Monday.

As she was running into the lobby of Two Commonwealth to catch up with Mattie, she heard Sam's voice behind her.

"The present doesn't have to be expensive," he said.

The Sunday game was scheduled for seven o'clock at Madison Square Garden. Josh explained it was done that way so that every pro football game except the Sunday night game would be over. Normally Molly wouldn't have been able to go to a Sunday night game, even in Boston. But this Monday would be one of four or five during the school year when there were teachers' conferences at the Prescott School. So when the Celtics flew on to Detroit after the game, Molly and Mattie would stay over in New York and take the shuttle home the next morning.

She was going to have half of Saturday with Josh in New York City and a lot of Sunday afternoon.

"Even though this is your first trip here," Mattie said during the ride to the hotel, "you've probably seen about as many sights in the big city as he has."

Molly had the guidebook Mattie had bought for her at the airport open on her lap.

"You're kidding, right?"

Mattie shook her head. "His idea of sightseeing is looking out the windows of the bus on the way to the Garden."

Molly pointed to her book. "He hasn't seen the Empire State Building?"

"Nope."

Molly turned another page. "Statue of Liberty?"

Shake of the head.

"He has to have seen Central Park."

"If he hasn't, we might have a shot," Mattie said.

The Sherry-Netherland was right across the street from the entrance to the park, Mattie showed her. Mattie described it as the Public Garden and the Boston Common times a hundred. She said that Josh had actually helped pick this particular hotel for the Celtics. He liked the idea that it really didn't look like a hotel in front but more like an apartment building, and because of where it was located on Fifth Avenue, it was hard for people wanting autographs to hang around on the sidewalk without the doorman rousting them.

"I know they let him call the plays," Molly said, grinning at Mattie. "But he gets to make the call on hotels, too?"

"You never heard people talking about the Cameron Rules?" Mattie said. "Sportswriters write that up all the time, saying they're more golden around the Boston Celtics than the Golden Rule."

For today, as much as she ever had, Molly felt like a golden girl, like the girl in *The Princess Diaries,* one of those happy-ending fairy-tale movies she liked to watch. Like she'd been picked out of the crowd and turned into some kind of royalty. Getting driven to the airport in a limousine. Getting met up by another limousine at LaGuardia Airport, the driver holding a sign with her name on it. She and Mattie staying in a suite that was right next door to Josh's suite, on a separate floor from all the other Celtics players. Looking out from the living room window at Central Park, which really did seem to go forever, wondering if somehow Josh Cameron had a view of a park wherever he went in his life. There was even a skating rink in this park, Wollman Rink, bigger than the one in Boston Common, so big it even had bleachers around it.

Molly pointed. "What's on the other side? Of the park, I mean."

Mattie said, "The West Side."

"Then what? I'm just trying to get my bearings."

"After the West Side comes what people here think of as the *real* West Side," Mattie said. "Of the whole darn country."

Josh had just called on Mattie's cell, telling her that the team had just landed, a little after three o'clock. Mattie talked to him for a minute, then motioned for Molly to come get on the phone.

"What do you want to do when I get to the city?" he said.

Molly thought about busting him a little, just on account of what Mattie had told her about his history with sightseeing. She might say she couldn't decide what she wanted to see first, the Statue of Liberty or Yankee Stadium.

Or maybe she'd just tell him she couldn't decide which museum she wanted to see first.

For once, she just came right out with it.

"I just want to be with you," she said.

It was so quiet at his end of the phone, she thought he'd run out of minutes.

CHAPTER 18

No hugs when Josh got to their suite.

The first thing he did was look at his watch.

He told Molly he'd made a reservation for them at a restaurant he liked a few blocks away, called the Post House. Saying there was a back door he could use, and a table tucked in the back of the restaurant.

"Sounds like going out to have room service," Molly said.

Mattie said, "Girl's got a point."

"Nobody will see us," Josh said.

"Whew!" Molly said, making a motion like she was wiping sweat off her forehead. "We wouldn't want *that* to happen."

"I thought we were losing the sarcasm."

"Slipped out."

"I'll see you back here about seven," he said.

It was five.

Molly said, "Wait, where are you going?"

"I've got a team meeting," he said. "And then some stuff I gotta do."

Molly looked at Mattie for help. But Mattie was frowning at Josh Cameron, like people do when they're trying to remember whether they recognize somebody or not.

"I thought we were going to get a chance to do stuff between now and dinner," Molly said.

"I'm sorry," Josh said. "This other stuff came up."

"But today's our one day in New York," Molly said.

"We've got tomorrow," Josh said.

"Gee," Molly said, "do you think it could be any better than today?"

Mattie, Molly saw, was still staring at Josh. He gave her a quick look and then turned away from her, almost like he was afraid.

"I can't help it if I've got things to do," he said.

"No," Mattie said. "You can't help it."

Molly didn't know what else she could say. So she went back over to the window and stared at Central Park, the skating rink in the distance she'd noticed before. Thinking about the day she'd imagined for herself in New York.

For the two of them.

"We'll have a great dinner," he said. "I promise."

Molly didn't even turn around.

"Whatever."

He made a sound like he was hurt, trying to make a joke out of the whole thing now, staggering backward. "I'm hit," he said. "By the *whatever* word."

Molly tried to give him the same frown Mattie had. "Is that supposed to be, like, funny?"

Josh reached into the pocket of his jeans, pulled out his wallet, took out a thick wad of cash, and handed it to Mattie. She looked down at the money and then up at him. "What is this, a tip?"

"More sarcasm," he said. "I thought you and Molly could go out. Go shopping or something."

"You just go," Mattie said. "We'll see you when you get back from that big meeting of yours."

"Seriously, take the money and shop," he said.

Molly wanted to tell him to take his money and do something with it, even if the suggestion wouldn't be very ladylike.

When he was gone and the suite was quiet again, Mattie said, "So what *do* you want to do, girl?"

Molly motioned her over to the window and showed her where the skaters were in the park.

Jen Parker had thought about being an Olympic figure skater someday, until she landed wrong at the junior nationals in Cincinnati when she was thirteen. She told Molly that knee surgeries in those days weren't as sophisticated as they became later. So you didn't come back, even at that age, as good as new from torn ligaments. She never got her chance to be one of those little ice princesses who were the stars of every winter Olympics.

But she still loved to skate, even though she used to tell Molly she was glad that they played loud music at most rinks, so people couldn't hear her bad knee making the kinds of noises only squeaky doors were supposed to make.

Molly would tell her, "You're still the best one out there by far."

"You're very sweet," she said. "Let's just say I'm the best one out there who's going so slow she looks like she's skating underwater."

In London they would skate at the Kew Gardens Ice Rink, at the Royal Botanic Gardens. Or at the Hampton Court Palace Rink, practically next door to Henry VIII's redbrick palace. Most of the time, they'd go to the Greenwich Ice Rink at the Old Royal Naval College, on the River Thames. Just the two of them. Molly never had any interest in competing. She would see some of the serious little-girl skaters at those places and wonder why they were even out there. They all had the same face on them. Like they'd all been sent to their rooms.

But she loved to skate. And got better at it, just by watching her mom. She even got to the point where she could do some basic spins and very tricky twirls, moves she'd only try if the Greenwich rink wasn't too crowded and she didn't feel like too many people were watching. When her mom's knee would start to bother her, she'd stop, go sit up in the small bleachers, and applaud silently when Molly would manage to get up in the air, pull off a spin, and land like a champ.

Anytime her mom said to Molly on a Saturday, "Okay, shop or skate?" Molly would always say the same thing.

"You even have to ask?"

She told Mattie all that after they crossed Fifth and made what felt like a pretty long walk to Wollman Rink. She was glad Mattie had ordered her to dress warmly, because it was getting colder now, winter cold, even in the last of the Saturday afternoon sunlight.

Molly skated in Central Park then, with Mattie watching her

from the bleachers. She started off slowly, not having skated since she'd gotten to Boston. Not really wanting to skate ever again, until now. But slowly she picked up speed and confidence, to the point where every time she passed Mattie, she'd try something. A jump. A spin. Some kind of flashy stop. Mattie would occasionally give her a thumbs-up, or just wave. She'd wave back.

She flew around Wollman Rink, and one time when she came around to where the bleachers were, Mattie was gone.

And Josh was there.

She started to skate over, but he made a motion for her to keep going.

"You're doing great," he said.

"How'd you find me?"

"Mattie has a way of yelling at me even in a note," he said.

"I didn't know she left you a note."

"She has secret powers," he said. "I thought you knew that by now. Now, go skate. I'll be the one in the stands for once."

Now he was her audience. She showed off as much as she possibly could, telling herself not to fall and end up looking like some dorky goof. She didn't want to look like a total klutz in front of him. She did even more spins and twirls and jumps than she'd done for Mattie. Josh was the one giving her the thumbs-up in approval now. Sometimes a double thumbs-up. She did one spin and looked up at him, and he made the motion like the players did sometimes, like he was trying to pump up the volume. All around her, she could see the lights of New York coming on.

An hour ago, he couldn't wait to get away from me, Molly

thought. Now he looks like he's having more fun than any-body here.

And boys were always saying they couldn't understand girls.

She skated until she thought she was going to drop. Picked up one more head of steam, like she was going to go right through the sideboards in front of him, put on the brakes like a pro, spraying ice everywhere.

He stood and applauded.

She did a skater's curtsy.

"Let's bounce," he said.

They walked back across Central Park and back down Fifth Avenue on the park side, toward the Sherry-Netherland. If people were noticing who he was, even in his knit-cap disguise, they didn't show it by bothering them. Maybe because Molly was with him.

He didn't seem any more comfortable with her here than he was anyplace else.

Molly thought, At least he's here.

He asked her what she thought of New York so far.

"I think I might have seen the best part of it back there," she said.

"I can't believe you and your mom never got here."

"She kept saying we'd do it at Christmas," Molly said. She felt her voice catch a little bit, like a sleeve she'd snagged on something. "She said when she was better we'd come to New York because I had to see the tree at Rockefeller Center at Christmas."

"Yeah," he said in a quiet voice. "She would say that."

"How come?"

"Because we were there once, the last Christmas before she went to Europe," he said.

"She never told me that."

"She told you everything *you* know about me," he said. "Just not everything *she* knew."

He pointed to a bench. "Sit down for a second," he said.

UConn was in New York to play a tournament called the Holiday Festival, between Christmas and New Year's. Just four teams, but still a big deal, because it was in New York, and in Madison Square Garden. If you won your first game, you made the final. UConn's first game was against Wake Forest, and if they won, they'd play Kansas, the number-one team in the country that year. Jen Parker wasn't supposed to be anywhere near New York. Her parents were still alive then, and she was supposed to spend the whole Christmas break with them.

Only she didn't want to.

"Why?"

"Because she knew how scared I was of coming to New York," he said.

"You?" Molly said. "Scared about basketball?"

"This wasn't just basketball," he said. "This was basketball at the Garden. They call it the Mecca. The Celtics have won a lot more than the Knicks ever did, but somehow it's still Madison Square Garden that's the capital of hoops. And I was sure that I was going to fall on my face. I kept telling that to your mom, and she kept telling me I was crazy, that I was going to be great and then everybody would know about me."

"But you didn't believe her," Molly said.

"Listen," he said, "when you're a kid, you always think there's somebody better. I thought I was good enough for my school then. But even if we got lucky in the first game, we had to go up against the number-one team in the next game. Which is where I'd *really* be found out."

"So what happened?"

"She left her parents a note, told them she was coming to New York to watch me play, jumped on a train."

"Sounds like something I'd do, kind of," Molly said.

"Just like Mattie says," Josh said, trying to imitate Mattie's voice. "Wonder where she gets it from?"

She smiled. He smiled. It was like somebody had cast a spell on them, just for this one day and night. She didn't want anything to break it. She didn't want the traffic noise to break it, horns that kept blowing every few seconds or the roar of the buses from the bus lane right in front of them. She didn't want anybody to recognize Josh Cameron, especially right now.

He told her how the UConn team was staying at the big Hyatt hotel near Grand Central Station. He got back there after practice, the day before the Wake Forest game, and there was a message from her mom in his room.

"It just said, 'Meet me at the tree,' " he said.

"What?" Molly said.

"Meet me at the tree," he said. "That was her message."

Molly looked up at him now, eyes wide. "Wow," she said, almost laughing.

"Wow what?"

"When she was getting sicker at the end," she said, "that's what she'd always say to me, to still make me think things were going to be okay. Meet me at the tree."

"In New York, there's only one," he said. "It goes up pretty soon, actually, but they don't light it until after Thanksgiving. They even make a TV special out of it now."

There had been a huge snowstorm overnight, he remembered. He said the only thing that would have gotten him out of his room that day would have been basketball.

Or her.

"Remember," he said, "no cell phones back then. She hadn't left me a number, or where she was staying. I had to go meet her if I wanted to see her."

He hadn't brought any boots. Just his one pair of high-top Converse sneakers, the blue-and-white version in those days because UConn wore blue. He had them, a sweatshirt, and the leather jacket she'd given him.

There he was, he said, slogging up Fifth Avenue in the snow, feeling his sneakers getting wetter and wetter. His gamers, he called them. Knowing he wasn't going to be able to find a pair that looked like them in New York in the next twenty-four hours, wondering how he was going to get them dry before the game.

He finally got to Rockefeller Center, soaking wet, freezing. Molly asked him where Rockefeller Center was. He said only about ten blocks down Fifth from the Sherry-Netherland. Which was roughly the same distance from the Hyatt that day, just coming from the other direction.

"I felt like a snowman by the time I got there," he said. "Looked like one, too."

"Was Mom there?"

"Of course not," he said. "That wouldn't have had any drama."

"She wasn't at the tree like she said?"

He said, "Let me finish."

There were all sorts of places, he decided when he got there, that could have technically been "at the tree." So he looked on Forty-ninth Street and Fiftieth Street and went back to Fifth. No sign of her.

"I figured I got stood up," he said. "It's still snowing like crazy, remember. So I'm not even paying attention to the skating rink underneath the tree, across from the NBC building there, the one they call 30 Rock."

"She said it's the coolest," Molly said.

A few blocks down, she could see the light from the big clock in front of the Sherry-Netherland. She didn't care what time it said. It was like they were in a whole different year now.

"All of a sudden I hear the Zamboni machine that cleans the ice," he continued.

He looked down. Somehow she had convinced the driver to clear a path for her. She had given him some story about how her boyfriend, the big basketball star, was coming and couldn't he please do this big favor for her, please, please, please?

So there the Zamboni guy was, driving up and back and clearing the snow while Josh wondered what the heck he was doing. Who in New York wanted to skate in weather like this?

"I found out who," Josh said. "Because out comes this crazy girl, arms out, going fast, like she was trying to fly."

"My mom," she said.

145

"Your mom."

He leaned over the fence and shouted to her that she was crazy. But he couldn't stop smiling at the sight of her. She yelled at him to get down there, look who was calling somebody crazy, the guy who was about to be the star of the Holiday Festival.

So he made his way downstairs and clumped across the ice in his wet sneakers, which felt as heavy as snowshoes by then.

She skated over to him. He said, "What are we doing here?"

And she said, "We're here because this is exactly where we're supposed to be. You. Me. Us. You're going to play the best two games you've ever played, and I'm going to watch you."

"You're sure of that?" he said.

Sure she was sure, Jen Parker said.

He wound up scoring forty points to beat Wake Forest and thirty-five against Kansas two nights later on the night at the Garden when UConn beat the number-one team in the country.

After the game that first night, Josh told Molly, he and her mom walked all the way back to Rockefeller Center from the Garden, snuck down to the ice. She said they had to do it for luck. He said they'd already won the game. She said she wasn't just talking about basketball.

They went to the same spot where they'd been in the snow and she told him that all happy endings had to have a place where they started.

"This is ours," she said.

Then she made him promise that he'd bring her back someday.

"Did you?"

Josh Cameron's eyes landed on the ground like some deflated ball.

"No," he said.

"No happy ending, huh?" Molly said.

And he said, "I stopped believing in those a long time ago."

CHAPTER 19

In the morning, Mattie said she was going looking for the nearest church.

Molly told her she was going to stay in the room until Josh got up. They had made a plan to have breakfast at a coffee shop around the corner, then for Molly to ride over to the Garden with him on the team bus. On the day of a game, the Celtics always had a light morning practice, called a shootaround. Josh had said he wanted her to see what New York's Garden looked and sounded like when it was empty, because it sure wasn't going to be that way later on.

"Don't go anywhere until Josh wakes up. Promise?"

"Promise."

Then Molly said, "I had a great time with him yesterday, Mattie."

There was a look on Mattie's face that was almost sad, even though Molly had told her what she thought was a happy thing.

"Know you did, little girl," Mattie said, then made sure she had a room key in her purse and left.

Molly watched a rerun of *Full House* on television, the show from when Mary-Kate and Ashley, the Olsen twins, were little and cute. She was about halfway through another *Full House* when she decided to call Sam. The show always made her think of him because he was the one who had gotten her hooked on it, not because he liked the Olsen twins, but because he said the actor who played the dad was cool.

"Bob Saget is a god," he would say every time they watched the show together, and every time he did, Molly would mention that she didn't know what planet Sam Bloom was living on.

Molly called Sam now, telling him she couldn't wait until Monday. She gave him pretty much a full play-by-play of her Saturday in New York with Josh Cameron.

"You're wearing him down," Sam said, "just as I predicted you would."

"It's not a fight," Molly said.

"Didn't say it was. But that doesn't mean you shouldn't be in there swinging." Then he said he couldn't believe she'd called in the middle of this particular *Full House*. It was the one where the great Saget got a cool girlfriend.

It was ten o'clock when the show ended. Time to get sleepyhead Josh up if he wasn't up already. She remembered the glad money in the back pocket of her jeans and decided she'd buy breakfast this morning and pay Sam back when she got home.

She made sure she had her key and walked across the hall, ready to ring Josh's doorbell.

Then she noticed the door was already open a little bit. She could hear loud voices from inside.

"You don't know what you're doing! That's the problem. Well, one of the problems."

"Bobby," Josh said. "You're going to give yourself a heart attack. That's provided we can find your heart."

"Oh, that's a good one. Ha ha ha. Look, I'm clutching my chest already."

Molly knew "Bobby" had to be Bobby Fishman, Josh's agent. Molly had talked to him a few times on the phone when he'd called the apartment at Two Commonwealth. The only thing he'd ever said to her was, "How you doing, kid? Is he there?"

Now, inside Josh's suite at the Sherry-Netherland, Molly heard him shouting.

"You're the one who's going to give me a heart attack. You not only bring her here, you take her for a walk in Central Park? So maybe somebody can take a picture of the two of you and put it on the front page of the *Post*?"

"You're making too much of this."

"Wait, I've got a better idea. Next time just take an ad in the papers. I'll even write the headline: 'Me and My Gal.' "

Molly knew she was eavesdropping, knew how much she hated it when she caught Kimmy trying to do the same thing outside the door to her bedroom when she was talking to Sam, especially lately.

But they were talking about her.

Josh said, "I'm going to ask you to do something I know is really hard for you, Bobby."

"What?"

"Lower your voice."

"You think this is funny?"

"No, but you are sometimes."

"I am not funny when I am creating an image for you more

150

wholesome than *milk*," he said. "I am not funny. I am *money,* my friend. And in case you have forgotten, I am about to sign you to the biggest sneaker deal in history because of your image, because you are anti-everything that sports fans don't like from all the bad boys. You are the good guy. Now, you tell me how it's going to look to the world if it finds out that Josh Cameron, single basketball star, never-married basketball star, has a kid?"

"When you put it that way, it doesn't look too good," Josh said.

"Thank you," Bobby said.

"Give me a rough estimate on how much this could cost me."

Like they were talking about buying a car or something.

"With what we're going to get if we switch to Nike? And the way they plan to promote you as the complete, total opposite of all the bad boys in sports? Believe me, you don't want to know."

Josh said, "I believe you."

The two suites, hers and Josh's, were both at the end of the hall. Molly looked down the hallway now. Nobody coming from the direction of the elevators. Nobody coming through the doors from the service elevator. She decided that if she saw somebody coming, she'd just whip out her key and go back into her own room.

Bobby Fishman lowered his voice slightly. "This isn't the way it was supposed to go."

"There was no way it was supposed to go," Josh said. "It is what it is."

Molly felt like she was hiding in the back of the Navigator again.

Bobby said, "Listen, I can tell you like the kid."

Molly couldn't hear what Josh said next.

Bobby said, "I'm sure she's going to grow up to be cuter than Hilary Duff."

Josh said, "She's not just cute. She's smart, she's funny, she's even got a mouth on her. She gets it."

"Well, here's what I don't get. If you don't think she's your daughter, how come you're treating her like one?"

Molly could hear herself breathing in and out, feel her head pressed against the cold door frame.

"I'm just treating her nice."

"No, pal, you're doing more than that. You're leading her on, is what you're doing. And making more trouble for yourself than I make you in endorsement money."

"I know what I'm doing."

"You pay me to know what you're doing."

"You're good, Bobby. But not that good. I can't just blow the kid off."

"So instead you act like you're trying to adopt her?"

Molly couldn't move, was frozen where she was, eyes closed. For a second, she pictured what it had been like at Wollman Rink every time she'd skate in front of him and he'd wave, the walk home on Fifth Avenue, the two of them sitting on the bench while he told her about meeting her mom at the tree. . . .

"Let's play this out," Josh said finally. "Say I tell her that I like her a lot, but I can't have her hanging around full-time."

"I could live with that."

"I'm not done. Say I do it in a way that makes her mad. Let's remember who her best friend's uncle is for a minute."

"A sports columnist for the *Globe.*"

"You don't think they could run to him and tell him that she's my kid?"

"She says she's your kid."

"You know what I'm saying, Bobby."

"You told me you don't believe she's yours."

"I don't."

Molly bit down hard on her lip.

"But you admit she could be," Bobby Fishman said.

"I told you that from the start," Josh said. "I gotta brace myself for that possibility."

Molly thought, The way people brace themselves for really bad news. Or a punch. Maybe Sam was right. Maybe this was some kind of fight, and Molly didn't know it.

"So for now, just my opinion, I gotta be nice to her," Josh said. "That way, it might not be as bad later when I tell her that the life I lead now and plan to lead for a long time, the one without a wife, it's not set up to have a family."

In her whole life, Molly had never once heard the word *family* sound like this.

Like a bad word.

Until now.

Amazingly, Bobby Fishman didn't say anything. Maybe he had finally run out of breath.

"Maybe that way," Josh said, "she'll understand better when I explain, if I have to explain, that the only thing that makes sense is shipping her off to boarding school."

Molly still wasn't moving as she started to cry, not even bothering to put a hand up to her face to get rid of the tears.

It was then that she heard Mattie's voice.

"Hey, little girl, what you doin' out here by yourself?"

Molly whipped her head around and saw Mattie at the other end of the long hallway, starting to take off her coat.

All Molly could do was shake her head. She didn't know whether Mattie could tell she was crying. She didn't care. She wasn't going back to her room. She didn't want to be in this hotel. She didn't want to be in New York.

She didn't want to be anywhere.

She turned the other way and noticed the door with the bright, red "Exit" sign over it.

Molly ran through the door, saw the stairway right in front of her, started taking the stairs two at a time, and jumped to the landing when she was halfway down the first flight.

Flying.

CHAPTER 20

She didn't know if Mattie, who was slow-moving even when she thought she was going fast, would go back to the elevators and try to beat her to the lobby that way. But after just one day at the Sherry-Netherland, Molly knew you usually had to wait for an elevator to come, especially if you were on one of the high floors like they were.

Or maybe Mattie had gone right into Josh's suite, thinking that something had just happened in there.

Either way, Molly had time to get away.

She wasn't going to let them catch her, Molly had made her mind up about that. She wasn't mad at Mattie. Mattie hadn't done anything. Mattie had already become her second-best friend in the world, after Sam. But Molly didn't want Mattie putting her arms around her today and telling her that things were going to be all right. Or that things were going to get better, child. That's what she called Molly in her sweet way sometimes. Child. But Molly was tired of being treated like one. And she hardly ever felt like one. She was tired of adults telling her that things were going to get better. They had been telling her that since her mom first got sick. First they said her mom was going to get better. That's what their friends in London said. Then Barbara told her that when they first got to Boston so the specialists at Mass General could take care of Jen Parker. She's going to beat this thing, that's what everybody kept saying.

Until she didn't beat it.

So her mom didn't get better, after all.

Then it was *things* that were going to.

What things? Molly wanted to scream at them sometimes, at the top of her lungs.

Because they couldn't possibly mean the things she was never going to get to do with her mom. Or the things she was never going to get to share with her. They couldn't mean the trip to the stupid tree in Rockefeller Center they were never going to make when she was better, because she never got better.

Now she didn't want anybody telling her that this was some big misunderstanding, that things were going to get better with Josh Cameron, who only wanted to be with her until he could figure out a way not to be with her.

She didn't want any adult, not even Mattie, the best adult she'd ever met outside her mom, telling her that she hadn't really heard what she knew she'd just heard from the father she now realized she was never going to have.

Whether he was her real father or not.

Maybe he planned on sending her back to Europe for boarding school. Maybe that was far enough away for him. Maybe he knew that worked since her mom had gone that far to get away from him once.

It was what Molly wanted to do right now. Get away from

him. He didn't want to be with her? Okay. She didn't want to be with him. She didn't want anybody, and she didn't need anybody, not even Mattie.

She didn't know how many flights she'd gone down, her mind moving about as fast as her legs. But she felt like she'd been running for a while. If Mattie had grabbed Josh, they could be in the elevator by now. Or even in the lobby waiting for her. When Molly jumped down to the latest landing, she went through the door there and looked at the number on the first door she came to.

Room 1011.

They been in 2111, she and Mattie.

She'd come down eleven flights. There was nobody in this hallway. Molly went halfway down it and pushed through the same double doors they had on their floor, the ones she'd seen the room service waiter come through. The service elevator was right there. Molly pushed the Down button and waited, bouncing impatiently on her toes. She didn't know where it opened up when it got to the ground floor, but there was no way it was at the small main lobby of the Sherry-Netherland.

When the doors opened, there was a room service waiter with a table in front of him and a messy tray on top of it. What was left of somebody's breakfast. The man had a white crewcut and a name tag that read "William." He smiled at Molly.

"Hey, hon," he said. "You don't want this one. The real elevator is right around the corner."

Molly Parker, thinking fast, wanting to ride down with him and right now, hit him with what she hoped was her brightest, widest, friendliest smile.

"I bet my big brother I could beat him down," she said. "And he always beats me at everything."

"What's your name?"

"Molly."

"Get in, Molly," he said, holding his finger on what must have been the door-open button. "What you got riding on the bet?"

"A whole stinking dollar," Molly said, making it sound like it was a fortune-and-a-half.

"We'll make this an express run," he said, turning a key in a little lock in front of him. "Skip the rest of the floors on the way down."

When they got to the bottom, it looked like they were in some basement.

"Is this the lobby level?" Molly said.

"Yeah, but over by the side door," William said. "There's a little service entrance nobody really knows about, on Fifty-ninth Street. The door's right there."

Perfect.

Molly sprinted for the door.

"Hey, where you going?" William shouted after her.

"Even if I beat him out of the buck," Molly said, "I still owe him two."

She went through the door and stood on the street, across from where she'd seen FAO Schwarz. Between her and the store, some kind of television show was being set up. Molly saw a banner that said "The NFL Today" being hung.

She took a deep breath. It was as bright and cold as yesterday had been. She was glad she'd put on her jacket before she'd left her suite, thinking she and Josh were going to go straight to breakfast.

Molly looked toward Fifth, over to her right. Madison, she knew by now, was left. If she walked over to the corner of Fifth, they'd spot her if they were standing in front of the hotel. She wasn't going that way. She started walking left, patting the wad of mad money in her pocket. Real mad money now. She walked fast toward Madison Avenue, which Josh had told her was one of the big expensive shopping streets in New York City. They had walked this way last night on their way to the restaurant, when Molly still thought she was in the middle of the best weekend of her entire life.

The life she'd had since her mom died, anyway.

She felt her pocket for her cell phone. Empty. She must have left it back in the hotel. In a little while, she'd get to a pay phone and call the room or Mattie's cell and tell her not to worry, that she was fine.

Then she'd call Sam, so the two of them could come up with a plan. That's what he called himself all the time. Sam, the man with the plan.

He'd know a way to get her back to Boston without asking for any help from Josh Cameron. Who had to brace himself for the chance that she might be his daughter the way he braced himself when he was going to get run over sometimes on the basketball court.

For now, Molly just wanted to be on her own. Might as well. She was going to have to get used to that.

So what if she was on her own in New York City?

Her mom had done it when she came to see Josh play that stupid game.

So could she.

There had been more people on the street the night before. Probably because it was Saturday night. More people, more cars, more noise as she and Josh had walked to Sixty-third Street, the street numbers on Madison going up one by one. As busy as New York was, with the noise it made even on a Sunday morning, Molly thought the streets were very organized.

In downtown Boston, she sometimes felt like she was caught in some kind of maze.

She walked up into the Sixties now, not having a real plan, waiting to talk to her man with the plan.

She was still mad. Steaming. Done with him for good, she was sure of that. But as she walked along Madison Avenue, Molly couldn't help feeling something else: Excitement.

She knew she should be scared, alone in what was still a strange city for her. Very strange, even though she had seen only this small part of it, the hotel to the park to the Post House, and what turned out to be the biggest and best banana cream pie that she had ever eaten. The only people she knew in New York were back at the hotel: Josh, Mattie, L.J., the rest of the Celtics. She tried not to think about that, or worry about Mattie being worried. It was only going to be for a short time.

Eventually she'd figure out how to get to Boston. Molly didn't know how much that would cost. She didn't know how much a lot of things cost. She was sure a plane would cost more than a hundred dollars. Maybe a train cost less. There had to be some way to take a train back. Maybe that was the way to go.

Sam would tell her what to do. Or Mattie could help, as long as she promised not to tell Josh what she was doing.

He was probably more worried about his game against the Knicks than he was about her, anyway.

What had her mom told her, over and over? The only two things he cared about were basketball and himself. Now Molly had found this out the hard way.

Better now than later, she told herself.

She had survived losing her mom. If she could do that, losing a dad she'd only had for a couple of weeks, one who didn't want her, would be a snap.

Adults were right about one thing: You could do pretty much anything you set your mind to.

She finally stopped at a restaurant on Madison called the Gardenia, one with a counter in back. Molly went back there, sat down, picked up a menu. The man behind the counter asked her in what sounded like a European accent—Greek or Italian, Molly thought—if she was waiting for her parents.

Molly almost said, I wish.

Instead she said, "My nanny. As soon as church is over."

Then she asked the man if she could have two eggs over easy with some home fries.

Breakfast for one now, not two.

She cleaned her plate, surprised at how hungry she was. When she finished, the man with the accent came over and asked if her nanny was late. Molly said church had probably run long today, and she'd wait for her outside. "Besides," she said to the man, "I live just over on Fifth."

Now she was in a movie. Not a happy-ending princess movie. Not "Annie." She didn't know how this one would come out, just that she was making it all up as she went along.

She went back out to the sidewalk. Everybody was always telling her how brave she was, and strong. Molly didn't have to be told, or tell anybody herself. She had only been afraid of one thing in her life, truly: losing her mom. After that, nothing was going to scare her very much ever again.

She wasn't afraid to go exploring New York a little bit now.

The night before, she had asked Mattie, who had grown up in New York—"little uptown part of town called Harlem," Mattie had told her—where the museum was that Sam had told her about, the one with the dinosaurs.

"Museum of Natural History," Mattie said. "Just over there on the other side of the park."

Molly, being the brave Molly, went over to the curb and stuck up her arm like she had lived in New York all her life, like this was the most natural thing in the world to do, hailing a taxicab. One pulled over right away, crossing about three lanes to do it. She jumped into the backseat and told the driver she'd like to go to the Museum of Natural History, please. Hoping he wouldn't ask for an actual address, that he was like one of the cabdrivers in London, who seemed to know anything.

"We'll go over to Fifth and then cut across at Seventy-ninth," the driver said, in another accent Molly couldn't place. "That okay with you?"

Molly said that was just fine.

The museum was open. She paid her way in and found the dinosaur exhibit with no problem. It was as cool as Sam Bloom had said it would be. She stayed there a long time, sometimes having the room to herself, alone with the dinos. She couldn't help thinking how much her mom would have liked it here. Her mom liked anything having to do with nature, with the world, used to talk about how much she loved going on camping trips, being out in the woods by herself when she was Molly's age and in something called Outward Bound.

Her mom always knew the names of flowers, and birds, and trees.

Molly was sure she would have gotten a kick out of these old dinos.

She wandered around a little more, then was back on the street. She went over to the window where she'd bought her ticket and asked what this part of New York City was called. "Upper West Side," she told Molly. "You from out of town?"

"Boston," Molly said.

"Boston?" The woman made a face. "The Celtics are playing here tonight. I hate the Celtics."

"Me too," Molly said.

Well, not all of them.

She walked around the Upper West Side now, past old brownstone buildings, pretty brownstone buildings, some of them looking as if they belonged on Beacon Hill, on Mount Vernon Street or Louisburg Square. Pretty and classy and old. Eventually she ended up on Columbus Avenue, at a big modern-looking place called the Reebok Club. Like the sneakers. With a Reebok sneaker store attached to it. People kept going in and coming out of the club, on their way to exercise, Molly guessed, or just having finished exercising.

At the corner of West Sixty-fifth Street, Molly asked a young woman pretty enough to be a model, in some kind of black tights and a halter top, how long a walk it was from here to Rockefeller Center.

"Well, it's about fifteen blocks down," the woman said. "Then a few blocks over." She closed her eyes, nodding, as if she were doing some kind of math problem in her head. "Figure, like, a mile and a half. Pretty long walk for a little girl."

Molly wasn't in the mood. "I'm not a little girl," she said. "I'm twelve."

"Sorry," the woman said. "My bad. I hated being called little when I was your age, too." She hunched down now, so she and Molly were eye-to-eye. "But can I ask you something without you biting my head off? Should you be walking around by yourself? 'Cause if you're asking where Rockefeller Center is, that means you're probably not from around here."

"I'm meeting my . . . cousins here," Molly said.

Keep making it up.

"They said they were going to take me down to Rockefeller Center, I just wanted to make sure I had the exact address. In case we walk when they get here."

"Cool," the woman said. "Too bad it's not a couple of weeks from now. You could see that big old tree when it goes up."

"Maybe we'll come back," Molly said.

Then she walked for what felt like an hour, downtown and then toward the park, finally seeing that she was on Fifty-ninth

Street, in front of a restaurant called Mickey Mantle's. She wasn't big on baseball, but even Molly knew who Mickey Mantle was.

"Before he got hurt," Sam told her once, "he was like a super-hero in baseball."

"I'll keep that in mind," Molly had said.

"There's things you gotta know, Mols," he said. "Mickey Mantle is one of them."

There was a clock inside Mickey Mantle's. It was after three now. Would Josh have left for the game yet? Molly wasn't sure. She knew he liked to get there early in Boston sometimes, but didn't know if that applied when he was on the road.

Didn't know and didn't care.

She decided to walk down Sixth Avenue instead of Fifth. When she saw a pay phone at the corner of Fifty-fifth and Sixth, she used some of the change she'd kept from breakfast, called information, got the number of the Sherry-Netherland, and asked for Mattie Charles's room.

"Is that Mathilda Charles?" the woman said.

"Mathilda?" Molly said, and almost laughed at Mattie's full name, never having heard it before.

It was the first time she'd felt like laughing all day.

"Yes," Molly said. "Please ring Mathilda's room." And giggled.

No answer.

She finally heard the voice mail click on, and when the voice on it finished her instructions, Molly said, "Mattie? It's me. Molly. Don't worry. I'll meet you back there after he leaves for the game, probably. Bye."

She hung up. Kept walking downtown on the left side of Sixth until she came to a place she'd heard about, Radio City Music Hall, looking big enough to take up nearly a whole block. Plastered all over the front, behind glass windows, were posters for the Radio City Christmas show, some of them showing pictures of the famous Rockettes, dressed up in what looked like Santa's-helper clothes, kicking their legs high.

The "world-famous" Rockettes, in the "world-famous" *Christmas Spectacular.*

They couldn't wait for Christmas in New York, that was for sure.

I can, Molly thought.

She couldn't think of one good reason why she wanted Christmas to come at all this year.

CHAPTER 21

$\mathcal{S}$he heard the skating rink at Rockefeller Center before she saw it. Heard the loud music—like elevator music, Molly thought—coming from somewhere below the street.

To her right as she came around the corner was another entrance to the NBC building, the one Josh had said was at "30 Rock." Only at this entrance it was called the GE Building, with this message over the doors: "Wisdom and Knowledge Shall Be the Stability of Thy Times."

Molly didn't know what GE stood for, but they could speak for themselves. She had all the knowledge she needed for one day, thank you.

She walked to the railing and looked down. There was the place where her mom had come to meet Josh Cameron. Before she knew what he was really like. Or before he turned into the kind of person she didn't want Molly to know. Of course, that was before Molly the brave one—or maybe it should be Molly the stubborn one, or just Molly the stupid one—had to find out for herself.

It was exactly the same as when you were little and found out you burned your hand by touching a hot stove, she thought.

The rink was much smaller than she expected. There was a little observation deck down to her right with tables and chairs. On the same level as the rink was a restaurant called the Sea Grill. Directly across from her was a sign that said that a man named John D. Rockefeller had built this whole place.

More knowledge and wisdom.

She didn't feel like skating today. She wasn't sure she wanted to skate ever again. If she really thought about it, she wasn't even sure why she was here. Maybe she just had to see for herself the place her mom had wanted so much for her to see, even without the big tree in place yet.

There was a man in some kind of security uniform, with a security hat on his head, walking past her with a cup of coffee, heading for the GE Building. Molly asked him where the tree went when they finally put it up. He pointed at the sidewalk underneath her feet. "Right about there, little girl," he said. "Few feet to your left, over by that star they drew into the sidewalk, makin' it look like one fell right out the sky."

"How big is it really?" Molly said.

The man pointed with his cup at all the skyscrapers around them.

"When I close my eyes sometimes, I picture it bein' as big as all them," he said.

Molly closed her eyes now, and imagined the biggest tree in the universe, reaching for the sky.

Reach for the sky, her mom had always told her, in everything you do. Then Jen Parker would laugh—her mom had that great

168

big loud laugh—and remind Molly to make sure that when she did, she wasn't always walking around with her head in the clouds.

"Because I could trip?" Molly asked her one time when they were packing up to leave London.

Molly, eyes still closed, remembered her clothes all over the bed that day, one big suitcase already full, another one open in the middle of all the clothes. Remembered the cloud that seemed to cross her mom's face when Molly asked the question.

" 'Cause you could trip," she said. "Like I did."

I did have my head in the clouds, Molly thought, with Josh Cameron. And this time I was the one who got tripped up.

Never again.

Forget about tripping. If you didn't count on anybody, they couldn't let you down, and they couldn't knock you down.

She leaned over the railing and looked down at the skaters. Next to her was a dad, waving to a girl about Molly's size down on the ice, the girl waving up at him the way Molly had waved at Josh at Wollman . . .

There was a big clock with old-fashioned Roman numerals above John D. Rockefeller's name. It was four o'clock by now. Josh was probably getting ready to leave the hotel for the game. She'd wait here a little while longer, maybe go get herself a hot chocolate down below, and then head back up Fifth Avenue toward the hotel. She was getting good at figuring out where she was in New York after just one morning and afternoon on her own. But anybody could have figured out how to get to the Sherry-Netherland. It was a straight shot up Fifth for ten blocks.

169

She had her key. She'd just go to the room and hope Mattie was there.

She wondered if Josh had even taken the time to look for her. Or worry about her. Or if he'd admitted to Mattie what he'd been talking about with Bobby Fishman.

She wondered if the great Josh Cameron could even admit to himself that he might have done something really rotten to her.

Probably not.

It was like her mom said. You couldn't be normal living in a world where nobody ever said the word *no* to you. Or had it been Mattie who said that? Sometimes in her head, it seemed like Mattie and her mom said the same type of things to her, trying to smarten her up.

She went back over, stood in the spot where the tree was going to go. Then she started walking back to the hotel.

She thought the Celtics would have left the hotel for the game by now. Josh had told her the bus usually left two and a half hours before the game. But she didn't see any buses as she crossed Fifty-ninth Street on Fifth Avenue.

Just Josh Cameron, walking down Fifth from the opposite direction, the same direction the two of them had come from Wollman Rink last night. He was wearing a gray hooded sweatshirt that had "Patriots" on the front, a pair of old blue jeans nearly faded to white. No leather jacket today. No knit cap. Just these huge wraparound sunglasses, about the biggest Molly had ever seen in her life, covering the top half of his face.

She stood there and watched him walking his pigeon-toed

walk, a beat too long. Because when he did look up, he looked right at her.

She didn't run.

She just turned and walked away from him, walking fast. She knew the Plaza Hotel was to her right, even though it was closed down right now because they were fixing it. Mattie told her all that, because Mattie knew how much Molly had loved the Eloise books about the Plaza. She looked back and saw him running.

Molly ran now as the light changed, heading for the Plaza, wishing there were some kind of fairy tale waiting for her over there, running toward the little park area in front of the hotel. She saw a man quietly playing a guitar and singing, saw other people sitting around on the benches out there, some drinking coffee, some reading the Sunday papers, some feeding pigeons. One man stood on a bench and took pictures of the horse-drawn carriages lined up near the entrance to Central Park.

She had always seen how fast he was on a basketball court. Now she found out herself.

"Molly!" he said.

He hadn't even waited for the light. He was dodging traffic like he was driving through it dribbling a ball. Of course not one car came close to him.

"Wait!"

She was thinking about running for the park instead when he got her by the arm.

"Do you want me to scream?" she said.

"No, I don't. And you don't want to."

"Yeah," Molly said. "You know me sooooo well."

"We need to talk."

"You did enough talking for both of us today, don't you think?"

"*That's* what I want to talk about," he said. "How much did you hear?"

"Enough."

"Whatever you think you heard, I'm sorry, I really am."

"Don't," Molly said.

It seemed like she was always telling him that.

"I mean it."

"You don't mean anything you say. You just say what you think people want to hear."

"That's not true."

Molly said, "And you don't know what true is, either. All you know how to do is play basketball. That's what's real with you, everything else is for show."

She shook off his arm. But Molly knew there was no point in trying to get away. She spotted one empty bench. He sat down next to her. There was a hot dog vendor set up on the sidewalk behind them. He asked if she wanted something to drink. She said it wasn't a picnic.

"Okay," he said, "how much *did* you hear?"

"Enough, I told you already."

"I don't know what that means."

"It means that you don't believe that I'm yours and that even if I am, you're just keeping me around until you can figure out a way to ship me off to boarding school."

He started to say something, but Molly cut him off. "Wait, I almost forgot. I have a question."

172

"What?"

"Do you have some good summer camp picked out, too? So you don't have to waste your precious time on me in the off-season, either?"

"Molly, listen to me. You misunderstood what I was doing with Bobby."

"No," Molly said, shaking her head hard from side to side, and squeezing her eyes shut when she started to feel more tears coming. She'd run again before she'd let him see her cry today. "No, no, *no.*" She sucked in some air and kept going. "See, that's my problem, I'm too smart for my own good sometimes, especially with grown-ups. Everybody says so. So, no, I didn't misunderstand. I understood perfectly."

"You are smart," he said. "And you're right when you say I sometimes only say what I think people want to hear. Because that's what I want to explain to you, that's what I was doing with Bobby before. That's what you heard. I was telling him what I thought he wanted to hear about you, just to get him off my back."

He reached over, tried to cover her hands with his big right hand.

Molly yanked her hands away like she'd seen a spider crawling toward them.

"C'mon," Josh said, "you must have done that at least once or twice in your life, even with your mom. Or Barbara. Or a teacher, maybe. Told them what they wanted to hear just so you could end the conversation and get out of the room?"

Molly looked up at him. He was smiling at her now, sharing this with her, smiling his TV smile, his magazine-cover smile, the one Mattie called his "money smile." He should have looked silly in those sunglasses. But he didn't. He just looked like the guy who always won over everybody in the end.

And then he messed up his hair.

What was Sam's expression? He was playing her.

He was turning on the charm like she was some reporter he wanted to win over.

"Molly, I'm sorry," he said. "I'm sorry I didn't explain to you about how I was trying to handle Bobby. I'm sorry I hurt your feelings." He leaned forward. "Come on, please tell me you accept my apology so we can get over to the game."

Grinned again. Ran his fingers through his hair again. "Pretty please?"

Molly stood up then.

"*Oh . . . my . . . God!*" she shouted at the top of her lungs, trying to be as loud as New York City.

All the people in the little park in front of what used to be the Plaza looked at them.

Molly smiled to herself.

"*I can't believe it's really you!*"

Trying to make herself sound like some ditz girl who'd spotted her favorite singer at the mall.

"*JOSH CAMERON!*"

"Molly, cut it out," he said, looking around, knowing that the damage was already done.

She looked right at him, then pointed.

"*JOSH CAMERON . . . right here on this bench!*"

Then she reached over, like she was stealing the ball from him in basketball, and pulled the sunglasses off his face.

Just because she felt like it.

All around, she could see people coming for them, some of the kids running.

"What do you think you're doing?" Josh said.

"What my mom did," she said. "Dumping you."

CHAPTER 22

I was just wondering," Barbara said. "Do you ever plan on talking to him again?"

It was the first week of December. They'd just had a huge snowstorm in Boston, one that surprised all the weather people on television, a storm that started late Sunday afternoon and didn't stop until Monday morning. Even got them a snow day from school.

Three days later, the Public Garden and the Common were still covered with snow, making it feel like the middle of winter already.

Molly had just gotten home from school, taken off all her snow stuff, gone straight upstairs to homework. Lots of homework.

She had looked up from her English assignment to see Barbara standing in the doorway.

"I just don't want to talk to him right now," Molly said.

"I don't want to say 'I told you so,'" Barbara said.

"So don't," Molly said.

"I really want to."

"I know," Molly said.

Barbara came in and shut the door behind her. Somehow, a minor miracle, Kimmy still didn't know the real story about Molly and Josh Cameron, not that it mattered much anymore, one way or the other.

Barbara lowered herself onto Molly's beanbag. "You're aware he keeps calling."

"Aware and don't care," Molly said. "Good rhyme, huh? Sam would be proud of me."

"I never really felt as if I got the whole story about what happened in New York," Barbara said.

She reached behind her, made the beanbag more like a chair, and settled back into it. Great. It must be some weird signal I give off, Molly thought, to all the Evans girls, that I'm ready to get down with some serious girl talk.

Except Molly never wanted to get down with girl talk. If she wanted to talk, she could call Sam. Or IM him. Or e-mail London friends.

"I just finally figured out that he didn't want me," Molly said. "And that there was nothing I could do to make him want me."

"I don't ever want to be put in the position of taking his side of things," Barbara said. "But it's pretty early in the process for you to decide that. And this is coming from somebody who thought the whole process was a bad idea from the start."

Molly closed her Mead Square Deal writing tablet, her favorite kind, and put it next to her on her bed with her pen on top of it. It was like putting down her weapons and surrendering. No matter how busy Molly tried to look, Barbara wasn't getting out of here one minute sooner.

Like mother, like daughter.

Or maybe it was the other way around.

"Process," Molly said. "You make it sound like I was trying to fill out some kind of application."

"Don't make this more difficult than it already is," Barbara said. "You know what I mean. In the best of all possible worlds, you and Josh weren't going to figure out the whole father-daughter thing in a blink."

She produced one of her signature Barbara sighs now. "Listen to me, talking about fathers and daughters like I'm some kind of expert on the subject," she said. "My dad and I still haven't figured things out, and we're starting to run out of time."

Molly nodded, like she understood completely, but didn't say anything.

Barbara said, "You can't ignore him forever. He *is* your father, after all. Even if he doesn't deserve you."

"He's really not my father," Molly said. "Not in any way that really matters." Molly couldn't help it, she made this groaning noise now, like the whole conversation had suddenly socked her in the stomach. "None of this matters."

"Of course it does."

"Not if I don't let it," Molly said. She looked right at Barbara, hoping she'd get the hint. "Or talk about it."

"You still talk to that housekeeper."

"Mattie," Molly said. "I talk to her on the phone sometimes, or she comes over if I tell her Sam and I are going to be hanging in the park."

"What does she think you should do?"

"Give him another chance," Molly said, "even though she got madder at him because of New York than I did. She says I have to cut him some slack because he has no idea how to deal with people. Girl people especially."

"But he has girlfriends," Barbara said, shooting Molly a disgusted look. "Lots of them, if you believe what you read."

"I asked Mattie about that," Molly said. "She says that most of them are so dumb, he doesn't have to talk to them, anyway."

"You really should talk to him," Barbara said.

"You're encouraging this now?"

"I'm not going to lie to you," Barbara said. "The idea of him being unhappy about something other than losing some silly game doesn't make me a bit unhappy. Believe me when I tell you that. But I made a promise to your mom to do everything possible to make *you* happy."

"I know I'm only twelve," Molly said, "but I think I've started to figure something out. You can only do that for yourself. If you expect other people to make you happy, you're always gonna end up disappointed in the end."

Finally Barbara got up. It looked like one of her yoga moves, the way she came straight up even though her legs had been crossed. She looked pretty proud of herself.

"Remember something," Barbara said. "We're moving in a few weeks. If you're going to try to patch things up, now is the time to do it. Before it's too late."

"Got it," Molly said.

"To be continued," Barbara said.

Boy, Molly thought to herself, I sure hope not.

She wanted to get all her writing done because the Celtics were playing the Bulls in Chicago later—it meant a late start, eight-thirty—and she wanted to listen to as much of the game as possible under the covers. She wouldn't admit to Barbara, or Mattie, or even Sam, she was still interested in the Celtics.

She might not miss Josh Cameron, but she missed the Celtics.

She missed being part of the team.

She did have a team of her own, at Prescott, getting ready to play the fourth game of their six-game season against Bartlett.

Which was, Sam pointed out at lunch the next day, a school even more precious than their own.

"How could that possibly be?" Molly said.

"More plaid," he said. "Lots more. I looked it up one time. I think Bartlett is the capital of plaid."

"Are you coming to the game?" Molly said. "You don't have to, you know."

"Can't make it until the second half," Sam said. "We've got some dumb yearbook meeting. But I will definitely be there, Miss Miss."

"Don't call me that."

Sam made an attempt to sound like a cat snarling and held up his fingers like claws.

"That was not a cat sound," Molly said.

Sam said, "I'll believe that when you pull back the claws."

"Sorry," Molly said. "Miss Miss was, like, a Celtics thing."

"I'll just write this off as you getting your game face on," Sam said.

"I don't even have a game face."

180

"Keep telling yourself that."

"What's that supposed to mean?"

"It means," he said, "that you've pretty much had your game face on since you got back from New York."

The Prescott-Bartlett game was scheduled for three-thirty. Prescott's record was only one and two, but it wasn't because Molly wasn't doing her part. She didn't take basketball nearly as seriously as some of the other girls on the team—or as their coach, Mr. Ford, the seventh-grade history teacher—but it didn't stop her from being the best they had, by far.

The day before, at practice, Molly had grabbed a rebound, dribbled through the rest of the team, and then instead of setting up their one play when she got across half-court, had seen an opening and driven all the way to the basket for a layup.

"I forget sometimes," Betsy Bender, one of the other guards, had asked Mr. Ford after the play. "What's Molly's position?"

Betsy Bender's entire contribution to the team, as far as Molly had ever noticed, was constantly yelling that she was open and waving for somebody to pass her the ball.

"Molly's position," Mr. Ford said, "is basketball player."

The more she played, the more she liked it. All of it. More than she ever thought she would. She'd basically only tried out for the team because she didn't want to wear the tights in ballet and didn't want to do drama.

She'd had enough drama in her life.

Basketball was different from skating, where it was all on you. In basketball, you had four other players to worry about, and she could see, just after a few games, how hard it was, juggling what was best for all of them and what was best for your-

181

self. More complicated than it looked. Sometimes what was best was shooting for herself, even though she didn't shoot nearly as often as she could. Sometimes it meant passing. Sometimes it meant passing to somebody you hadn't passed to in a while just to make sure that player didn't forget she was still on the team.

That was Mr. Ford's big thing, keeping everybody involved.

Little by little, she was figuring out the best way to do it. And while she would not ever admit this to Mr. Smarty Pants Sam Bloom, the way that made it easiest for her was imagining that she was Josh Cameron.

Because all the things Mr. Ford talked about, when he was giving them his daily speech about playing basketball "the right way," Josh did every single time he was on the court. The basketball "values" that Mr. Ford held sacred? All you had to do was watch Josh play to understand them, because they were right there for you, as plain as day. Playing on her first basketball team, that hadn't been the crash course for her in basketball. Watching Josh was her crash course.

Even though she acted like she didn't watch—or care—anymore.

The Bartlett bus got to Prescott late, a few minutes after four. When Molly heard the applause from the layup line, she assumed that the parents in the stands, impatient for the game to start, were just being sarcastic.

Only the applause wasn't *for* the Bartlett players.

It was coming *from* them.

Molly said to Mr. Ford, "Shouldn't they wait to do something good in the game before they cheer for themselves?"

Mr. Ford said, "They're not cheering for themselves. Check it out."

Betsy Bender said, "Isn't that one of the Celtics?"

Molly almost didn't want to look. She suddenly felt her heart beating inside her chest, was sure that her teammates could hear her heart beating inside her chest.

He'd come here?

Without even giving her a heads-up?

She took a deep breath, then looked at the seats by the other basket where Mr. Ford was pointing, deciding how she wanted to play it when he saw her looking up at him.

Only it wasn't the him Molly thought it was.

"Miss Miss!" a familiar high-pitched voice boomed out from the upper seats, in Prescott's old-fashioned gym.

Molly smiled.

There was L. J. Brown waving at her.

And Mattie.

Molly couldn't help herself. She ran straight down the court, past the players on the Bartlett team, and jumped right into L.J.'s arms.

She hadn't been this happy to see anybody—with the exception of Sam Bloom—since she'd put her game face on and kept it on after New York.

L.J. squeezed her tight and said, "Looks like Miss Miss has been missin' me as much as I've been missin' her."

"More," she said.

She pulled back her head and looked over at Mattie, who winked.

Molly said, "What're you guys doing here?"

"Mattie told me what happened."

Molly gave Mattie a raised eyebrow. Sam said it was one of her best looks, right up there with the innocent look she'd give teachers when she'd get Sam giggling in the back of class sometimes. "Told you what?"

"She just said the star made you mad, so mad you run off on him in New York. And that now you don't want to come around anymore."

Mattie winked again, then made a motion like she was zipping her lips.

"I thought you guys had a game in Cleveland tonight," Molly said.

"Game's here, Miss Miss. Thought you knew the schedule by heart."

"But usually when they give you a back-to-back, you have the home game first. Or they're both on the road."

"Schedule maker gave you a little head fake there, didn't he?"

Molly said, "Maybe I was just more worried about my game than yours."

He laughed his laugh. "Maybe I am, too."

"So Mattie told you about my game, too?"

"I called the star 'bout this appearance we got tomorrow at the State House," he said. "Mattie answered. I said, 'Whassup with my girl?' Meanin' you. Mattie told me about New York first, then she said, wait a second, let me check something, my girl might have a school game today."

"You know my schedule?" Molly said to Mattie.

"Along with everything else," Mattie said.

"Molly!" Mr. Ford yelled from down in front of the Prescott bench. "Would it be rude or some kind of imposition if I asked you to join us?"

"Be right there, Coach," she yelled. Into L.J.'s ear she whispered, "Be*have.* I mean it."

"What?" he said, acting offended. "You think I don't know what manners to put on at Miss Miss's School for Good Girls and Boys?"

She jumped down and sprinted back down the court. Feeling pumped for the game now. Feeling better about things than she had since she got back from New York. In the huddle Mr. Ford said, "L. J. Brown is a *friend* of yours?"

Molly gave him and her teammates her best possible no-biggie shrug.

"We go way back," she said.

After that, Bartlett had no chance against Miss Miss's School for Good Girls and Boys. It wasn't just that Molly played her best game, by far, with L.J. and Mattie watching. It was more than that.

On this day, Molly was doing things on the court she didn't even know she could do.

She wasn't showing off. Well, maybe a little bit. There *might* have been a couple of passes where she looked one way and threw the ball the other. And maybe a couple of Josh Cameron step-back shots when she might have held her arm up in the air a second extra, the way she did when she was playing H-O-R-S-E with L.J.

But in Molly's mind, it was all right. It wasn't so much the showing off as having someone to finally show off for, that's the way she looked at it.

Prescott was ahead by twenty points at halftime. She went up and got L.J. then, because the two coaches had decided it would be a cool thing for him to come down and sign autographs for the players on both teams. And the teachers who had suddenly appeared out of nowhere. And the moms and dads and siblings in the gym.

Even Kimmy Evans had shown up after ballet.

"Okay, it's official," Kimmy said. "I want to be you when I grow up."

Was she being sarcastic? Or just Kimmy? It was one of those times when Molly wasn't sure.

"No, you don't," Molly said.

"What, you don't think I'd make a good team mascot for the Celtics?"

"I'm not their mascot," Molly said. "I'm not their anything these days."

Kimmy gave a little nod at L.J. "Could've fooled me," she said, and got into the autograph line.

When L.J. finished, he came over and sat down with Molly behind the Prescott bench. "Gonna call you Star from now on," he said.

"I've learned from the best," she said.

"J.C., you mean."

"Uh uh," Molly said. "I learned my best moves from L.J."

He put out his hand so she could give him five and said, "That's what I'm talkin' about!"

By the time the fourth quarter started, Prescott was ahead by thirty and Mr. Ford had ordered Molly and her teammates to pass the ball at least five times before they even thought about shooting. And had told Molly to stop shooting entirely, which was fine with her. Halfway through the quarter, he finally took her out for good. And for this one very awesome moment, Molly felt like one of the Celtics, one of those games when they had such a big lead that Coach Gubbins would take out his first stringers one at a time, so each one of them could get a cheer all to himself.

She was worried that L.J. might make a fuss, being L.J. But he still had his manners on. He applauded along with the other people in the gym. When Molly caught his eye, he just smiled and nodded. She noticed that Sam was with him. He stuck two fingers in his mouth and whistled, just to make sure Molly, and everyone else, knew he was in the house.

When she changed back into her school clothes after the game—no girl on the team had ever taken a shower after a game that Molly knew about—L.J. and Mattie and Sam were waiting for her in the gym.

Mattie said, "I called Miz Evans, and she said she'd call Sam's mom. L.J. and me will run you both home."

Sam answered for both of them, of course. "We're good with that."

The Prescott School was on Exeter Street, around the corner from where Niketown was on Newbury. L.J.'s own Navigator—bright red—was parked right in front of Niketown, as if the No Parking sign was a meter. He pointed his keys at it, and the doors unlocked.

Molly opened the back door on the sidewalk side.

Before she could get in, Josh Cameron stepped out.

"You're not the only one who can stow away in somebody's car," he said.

Molly shook her head.

"You don't give up, do you?" she said.

He said, "Where do you think I get it from?"

CHAPTER 23

They all stood on the sidewalk until Sam said, "I'll sit over by the window. Mols, you can get in the middle in the back."

Molly thought about going right back into the school and calling Barbara, but she knew it wouldn't do any good, so she got in next to Sam.

Mattie sat up front with L.J.

"You guys knew about this?" Molly said.

"I did," L.J. said.

"And you helped him out . . . *because?*"

"Because I'm a good teammate," he said.

"You're my *friend*," Molly said.

"His, too," L.J. said. "And his first."

"What about you, Mattie?" Molly said.

"You two need to talk this out," Mattie said. "So we're gonna go home so you can talk it out. Then whatever you decide after that—and I mean you, little girl—that's just fine with me."

L.J. turned around. He still hadn't turned the key in the ignition. "It's the right thing for everybody, little girl." He put up

189

one of his huge hands. "I know, I know, you don't think you're little. But you are to me."

L.J. looked hard at her now and said, "Fathers and daughters need to talk."

Molly whipped her head to the side and looked at Josh. He shook his head.

Then she looked at Mattie. "Did you tell?"

L.J. said, "Nobody had to tell me, Miss Miss. It was me told them."

Quietly, Sam said, "We're having some fun now."

"I got eyes," L.J. said.

Molly slumped in her seat. "This isn't a fair fight," she said.

To Josh she said, "Do you have anything to say?"

"Just waiting my turn."

Mattie turned all the way around in her seat, reached over the armrest, and offered her hand, which looked like it could have fit into L.J.'s hand the way a penny would have. Molly took it. As usual, Mattie's hand felt as warm as the inside of a soft glove.

"We've gone way past what's fair and what's not in this world, haven't we?" she said.

Now L.J. turned the key and put the Navigator in gear.

They dropped off Sam first. By the time they got to Two Commonwealth, it was five-thirty and getting dark, the kind of dark at that time of day that made you know how fast winter was coming on.

Josh and Mattie got out first. Molly just sat there in the back-seat.

L.J. turned around and smiled at her one last time and said, "Be*have*."

She got out. As she and Josh and Mattie got into the elevator, Molly said to Josh without looking at him, "Shouldn't you be at the game by now?"

"It's late, because it's on TNT tonight," he said. "So we've got some time."

"Maybe you do," Molly said, staring straight ahead and looking at the numbers. "I've got a paper due."

"You're not going to make this easy, are you?" Josh said.

"It's like L.J. always says," Molly said, still watching the floor numbers, like it was the most interesting thing she was going to see all day. "It is what it is."

She almost blurted out in the elevator, right as the doors were about to open on the first floor of his place, that she was moving to Los Angeles and what did any of this really matter?

But she didn't. If this was it for the two of them, she might as well hear him out. She pretty much knew what she wanted to say to him. Which was basically that nothing he was going to say was going to change her mind. Her mom had always told her to trust her heart. And even that first day, when he had peeled rubber and left her there in the parking lot, she knew in her heart— a part of it, anyway—that he didn't want her around.

When they all got inside, Mattie said she was going to leave the two of them alone, but did Molly want anything, a snack or a drink, before she went upstairs?

There wasn't a single time Molly had ever been here when Mattie didn't act as if Molly must have just gone three or four days without eating and might be starting a hunger strike.

"You know what I'd really like?" Molly said. "A ride home."

"I'll take you when we're done," Josh said. "We can ride over or walk."

"Mattie can take me."

To Mattie Josh said, "We'll figure this out later and call you."

He went to the kitchen, came back with one of those small bottles of Coke, because he knew Coke in a small bottle was Molly's favorite.

"I'm not thirsty," she said.

"Just in case you get thirsty," he said.

"Why are we here?"

"Because Mattie's right," he said. "The way she's always right." He gave her one of his lopsided grins, where it was like one half of his mouth tried to fall right off his face. "The way your mom was always right."

"Right about you," Molly said. "She didn't want to be with you in the end, and she didn't want me to be with you ever. I should've listened to her."

"Me too," he said. "Listened to her, I mean."

"About what?" Molly said.

"Believing in stuff," he said.

Molly knew how big her mom was on believing, and how if you did, you could make things come true. She believed and kept believing, even when she had to know she was wasting her time believing she was going to get better.

"Mom thought faith was like magic," Molly said.

She looked out the window. The tallest trees in the Public Garden were swaying, almost in slow motion, in a big wind. Josh didn't seem to be in any hurry to get to his game, and so she wasn't going to worry about it. It was like L.J. had said once, that the only "on time" that mattered with Josh Cameron was "game time."

"Your mom told me once," he said, "that if I'd just believe we'd always be together, then we'd always be together."

"Then you blew it."

"Yeah," he said. "I blew it."

Molly had been watching the trees and the lights beyond them while she talked to him. Now she took a sip of Coke, right out of the bottle. It was still cold.

"That's all you have to say?" Molly said. "You blew it?"

Josh said, "I didn't figure out until after she was gone that she was pretty much the best thing that had ever happened to me."

"I never asked you before. How come you never went after her?"

"The truth?"

"No," she said, "lie to me a little more."

"Wow," he said.

"Yeah," Molly said. "Wow."

"It was my stupid ego," he said. "My jock ego. She didn't want me? Fine. Then I didn't want her."

Now Molly was watching him. Almost like I'm guarding him, she thought to herself. Waiting for him to fake her out again, the way he had just about every single step of the way.

But she wasn't letting her guard down for a second.

Even if he actually seemed to mean what he was saying for once.

"She was gone," he said, "and I was in the pros."

"You had turned into *Joooooooosh Cammmmmmmmeron!*" Molly said, trying to say his name the way the announcer at the Banknorth Garden did.

"Pretty much," he said. "We weren't just living in different countries, it was like we were living in whole different worlds. And I didn't know what to do about that. So I ended up doing nothing."

Molly said, "And now, what, I'm supposed to feel sorry for you?"

"You? Never in a million years."

" 'Cause I don't."

He put his feet up on the coffee table, which would have made Mattie yell at him. She noticed he was wearing new sneakers. Nikes for a change. Molly had to admit they were cool-looking.

"We have more in common than you think," he said.

"Right."

"No, really. We both figured out a way to live without your mom."

"I haven't," Molly said.

"You have," he said. "More than you think, anyway."

"I'm never going to." She took another big swallow of Coke, squeezed her eyes shut.

A way to stop tears before they started.

"Listen," he said.

"I'm all ears."

"I'm not saying things between us could ever be the way you want them to be."

194

Molly cut him off.

"You don't want them to be anything," she said. "I heard you that day in New York. You've just been trying to buy yourself some time, or whatever, to figure out a nice way to get me out of your hair. And don't tell me you were just saying that, or you can call up to Mattie right now."

"Okay. I won't."

"Just so we're clear."

"Crystal." He leaned forward on the couch. "But I got clear on something else the last couple of weeks," he said. "I kind of like having you around."

"Wow," she said, mimicking the way he had said it. "What a compliment."

"I mean it."

"Even when you were with me," Molly said, "you weren't with me."

"That's not true."

"I was there, remember? Or maybe you didn't notice, on account of you were on your cell. Planning your escape route."

"I was trying to figure it out."

"You weren't trying at all."

"You're wrong," he said. "If I wasn't trying, you wouldn't have been hanging around in the first place."

She looked at him. Really looked at him. Watching for one of his fakes. For him to start messing around with his hair.

But he didn't.

All of a sudden she didn't want to tell him there was no point to this. Because they were doing what Mattie wanted them to do, which meant really talking about stuff. The way they had only one other time, when they were walking back to the hotel from Wollman Rink.

And how did things work out *that* time? she was thinking.

"Molly?" he said.

"Huh?"

"Where'd you go? I think I lost you there for a second."

"You lost me a while ago."

"I don't think so. If I did, you wouldn't be here with me now."

Her head was starting to spin again. She had enough to think about for one day.

"I need to go," she said.

"Yeah," he said. "With me. To the game."

"It's going to end too late."

"Only makes it better."

For once, he was right.

Barbara wasn't thrilled with the idea, because of when the game was starting and because they'd sprung the plan on her so late, but in the end she decided to let Molly go. Knew she had to, for Molly's sake.

"Be careful, though," she said. "He's just trying to turn on the old charm."

"I'm not making a big deal out of it," Molly said.

"We'll see," Barbara said.

We'll see, Molly knew by now, was part of some code for grown-ups, where they said that instead of what they really wanted to say, which was that you had no idea what you were talking about.

"It's just one game," Molly said. *"You'll* see."

She had told Josh that the only way she was going was if Sam could go, too. Mrs. Bloom was about as happy as Barbara was with the late start, but she decided to make an exception. The plan was for them to sleep up in Mattie's apartment when they got back from the Garden.

Josh drove. When they picked up Sam, Josh said to him, "You probably didn't expect to see me again so soon."

"Or ever," Sam said. "But when you're Molly's friend, you kind of learn to go with the old flow."

When they were in their seats at the Garden, behind the bench, Sam said, "Okay, how did we go from him stinking more than rotten eggs to courtside seats?"

"He tried today," Molly said. "Waiting in L.J.'s car, the stuff we talked about." She threw up her hands. "He tried."

"So now you're buying his gig?"

Sam had his own language sometimes. There was just no way around it.

"Gig makes me want to giggle," Molly said.

"Cute," he said.

"Thank you."

"I don't suppose it came up that you are moving in, oh by the way, a few weeks?"

"It didn't," Molly said. "I'm not giving him a deadline, because I don't want him to be pressured into thinking about him and me in a way that he wouldn't have thought about him and me in the first place."

"I actually followed that."

"It wasn't that hard," Molly said.

Sam said, "It's like the test."

"You mean the DNA one?"

"Yup."

"The one I was going to use before I didn't want to use it," she said.

"Yup."

"I guess it is," she said. "I want him to figure this out for himself, the way I did."

"He has to want you as his daughter because he wants you as his daughter, not because anybody made him made him want to do it," Sam said. Then he shook his head a couple of times, like he was dazed and confused suddenly. "Oh, my God," he said. "Now I'm starting to talk like you."

On the floor in front of them was their first disgusting Sam snack of the night. What he called his "pregame meal." Nachos. Two hot dogs. Curly fries. Onion rings. Two Cokes.

Molly said, "If he only does something because I'm leaving, it doesn't count."

"With you," Sam said. "It doesn't count with *you*."

"Right," she said.

Sam Bloom, her best friend, the frog she thought of as a prince, didn't turn his head, just kept watching the Celtics warm up as he said the next thing.

"How come we never talk about what you moving to LA is going to do to you and me?" he said.

This wasn't the funny Sam now. This wasn't Sam playing.

This was serious.

Molly gave him as serious an answer as she could.

"Because if I don't talk about it," she said, "then that's a little while when I don't have to think about it."

She took his hand, and for once he let her without yanking it away.

"I think about it all the time," he said.

"I know."

"You gotta tell him, Mols. If you tell him you're leaving, I bet he won't let you."

"No."

"Molly's Rules," he said. "Like the Cameron Rules."

The horn sounded, which meant the game was about to begin.

"Less than three weeks until Christmas," he said. "It's not enough time."

"What do you call it when you put up a crazy shot and try to beat the buzzer?" Molly said.

"Firing up a prayer," he said.

CHAPTER 24

*T*he Celtics went on the road for a week right after that, one game in Utah and then three in Texas against the Rockets, Spurs and Mavericks.

Now it was the last full week before Christmas, and Josh still had no idea that the Evanses were packing for the move to Los Angeles. Molly didn't take any chances when the Celtics came back off the road, never letting Josh pick her up at 1A Joyless, always waiting outside when he'd pick her up or working it out that she'd go meet him at his place.

Mr. Evans and Barbara had decided to hold off on selling their Boston home for now, because Mr. Evans said there was a chance he could be coming back in a couple of years. The most his bank had asked for from him was a two-year commitment. They would rent it out instead.

"Nothing is forever," he said to Molly one day.

Tell me about it, Molly told herself.

Once the Celtics got home from Texas, they had three straight games at the Garden. Molly got to go to a couple of practices on the off days, got to goof around when they were done and play H-O-R-S-E with L.J.

Only this time Josh played, too.

He killed them both.

When it was over, he looked at Molly and L.J. and shrugged. "Sorry," he said. "I don't even like losing coin flips."

L.J. looked at Molly.

"That's why he's him, and the rest of us is the rest of us," he said, then laughed his laugh.

The second day she was at practice, Coach Gubbins did something he said the great Celtics coach Red Auerbach used to do: Divided the team up into the big guys and the little guys. Not that Molly thought of any of them, Josh included, as being particularly little.

Red Auerbach had told Coach Gubbins that when he used to do it, the little guys usually won, even though one of his big guys was Bill Russell. Molly sure knew who that was by now, having heard the coach talk about him enough. Bill Russell had played on Celtics teams that had won eleven championships in thirteen years and was the greatest Celtic of them all, greater than Bob Cousy or Larry Bird. Even greater than Josh Cameron, though the coach would never say that too loudly when Josh was around. Russell's number, six, was one of the retired numbers up there at the top of the new Garden, just the way it had been at the old Garden.

Coach said his Christmas present to Molly was that she could coach the little guys.

"Maybe they'll listen to you," he said, and winked.

Josh and the little guys won. When it was over, he said to Molly, "You ask me, coaching was the difference."

Molly said, "It might have been the guy I had handling the ball."

Josh tapped her closed fist with his. "That's what they all say," he said.

It was a great week. One day after school, they snuck into a movie, just her and Josh. He got the tickets beforehand, worked it out with the manager, and the two of them sat by themselves in the balcony.

One night, even though it was a school night, he ordered in pizza from Upper Crust, and he let Molly pick the movie. She went with her all-time favorite, *Miracle on 34th Street*, the black-and-white one.

They ate pizza, and he watched the whole movie with her and didn't get up to answer the phone or make a cell phone call one time.

Molly still hadn't told Mattie about the move. And she had sworn Sam Bloom to secrecy under penalty of what she threatened would be, in Sam-speak, a severe beatdown.

"I'm not afraid of you," Sam said, then quickly added, "Well, maybe a little."

"Those are my terms," she said.

"How come this whole gig has to be on your terms?"

"Because," Molly said to him, "up to now practically nothing that's ever happened to me has been on my terms."

Five days before Christmas now. Six until they moved.

There was a Saturday game tomorrow, a day game, and they were supposed to have dinner at Two Commonwealth, her and

Mattie and Josh. Then the Celtics had a few days off before playing one of the big nationally televised games of the season—the Christmas Day game against the Knicks.

She'd tell him at dinner. Tomorrow.

Then she'd find out whether the week they'd just spent together was real or not. Or whether this was just more make-believe with him. She'd find out whether he wanted her to stay or go. What if he'd already found out somehow that she and the Evanses were moving, and he was only being this nice to her because he knew he'd be rid of her soon? What if he was fine being her friend as long as she had another home to go to—what he thought of as her real home?

What if?

That night, she spread her mom's letters around her on the bed and went through them until she found the one she was looking for, one her mom wrote not long after they got to Boston.

"We can what-if ourselves to death, pardon the expression," her mom wrote. "But what-if never does anybody any good. All any of us ever have, sweetheart, is one thing, and we better make the most of it while we can: What *is*."

She would tell him tomorrow what was. That the Evanses were moving to Los Angeles, but she wanted to stay with him. Him and Mattie. Wanted the three of them to be as much of a family as they could. Molly was sure Josh's fans would understand, once they knew the real story. He hadn't lied to anybody about anything. He hadn't known that he ever had a daughter. Now he knew, and he wanted her to be with him.

If he wanted her to be with him.

All Molly could do was try. If he still couldn't handle the idea of being a real dad to her, if he wanted her to go, well, she'd at least have given it one last shot.

She organized her letters, put them back in the box, shut off the light, fired up a real prayer about tomorrow, and went to sleep.

CHAPTER 25

*T*he Celtics won their Saturday game easily over the Miami Heat, which Molly thought was one of the funnier team names. She wondered what they did about a team mascot. How did somebody dress up as heat?

Her friend L. J. Brown was the one who was hot on this night, scoring thirty-two points, the most he'd had in one game all season. Josh, perfectly happy to keep feeding L.J. the ball, ended up with twenty assists, the most he'd had in a game in two seasons, according to Sam the stats guy.

Molly told Sam once that if his head spilled open, numbers would come tumbling out. Along with nacho cheese. Lots and lots of nacho cheese.

"I should be so lucky," Sam had said.

When the game was over, Mattie said that the hired car was waiting outside near the players' parking lot to take them home. Josh and the rest of the Celtics players had a stop to make first, at Children's Hospital Boston, where they were all going to play Santa Claus for the kids there.

He said that he'd be home by seven-thirty, eight at the latest, and he and Mattie and Molly could still have dinner together.

"No later than eight, mister," Mattie said, wagging what Molly always thought of as the finger of death at him.

"Cross my heart," Josh said outside the locker room, actually crossing his heart.

"No need to finish the rest of it," Mattie said, cutting him off. " 'Cause you *will* die if you're late for my pot roast."

They dropped Sam off first. Then Molly asked if she could stop at home because she wanted to pick up the Christmas presents she'd wrapped for Mattie and Josh.

"Does he know we're supposed to exchange tonight, and whatnot?" Mattie said.

"We don't have to exchange," Molly said. "I just want to give you guys mine."

Then she added, "You guys have given me a lot already."

Now, she thought, I just want him to give me a yes.

When they got to 1A Joyless—by now she knew she was going to think of it this way to the end—Molly unlocked the front door with her key, knowing that Mr. Evans and Barb and Kimmy had gone to a real performance of *The Nutcracker*, at a real theater. She grabbed the two presents from the bottom drawer of her desk, raced down the stairs, locked the door behind her, and got into the backseat with Mattie, smiling to herself as she did, picturing them opening their presents, picturing the way she was sure the night was going to go.

Mattie said to Molly, "Is there something you know that I ought to know, my girl?"

"Tell you later," Molly said.

"You keepin' secrets?"

Mattie looked at her, smiling at her the way Molly imagined a grandmother would, from underneath her black beret. Molly knew she was going to love the red one—cashmere—she'd bought with all her saved-up allowance and birthday money the day she'd gone Christmas shopping for Mattie, Barbara, Mr. Evans and Kimmy at Louis, a big clothing store on Newbury Street around the corner from Two Commonwealth.

"No secrets," Molly said.

"When I think he's keepin' a secret on me, I make him tell me," she said.

Molly smiled at Mattie, and then used a Sam line on her. "I'm not afraid of you," she said, then quickly added, "Well, maybe a little."

They both laughed. She pressed her cheek into Mattie's coat, loving the scratchiness of it, feeling the warmth of it and Mattie at the same time, feeling as safe and snug with her as she felt anywhere.

Thinking to herself that everything finally felt right.

When they got back to Two Commonwealth, Mattie said she had some shopping to do before the stores closed.

"Shopping for who?" Molly said.

"Never mind."

Then she said she'd be back in about an hour. Molly said she wasn't going anywhere, settled in on the couch, found some episodes of *Full House* she'd put on Josh's TiVo once she figured out how to operate it.

When the doorbell rang two minutes later, she just figured Mattie had forgotten her purse or keys or something.

Molly was already mimicking Mattie as she opened the door, talking to her the way she talked to Josh, saying, "You'd forget your head it wasn't attached to your shoulders—"

Only it wasn't Mattie.

It was Bobby Fishman.

"Remember me?" he said.

He was talking fast right away, almost like he'd started in the elevator. He told Molly he'd seen Mattie walking around the corner to Arlington as his cab dropped him off. He told her he'd left Josh and the guys at Children's Hospital. Told her Josh was going to be there a little longer than he originally planned. The kids had prepared a Christmas show for the players, and they all had to stay.

Told her all that in what felt like ten seconds.

"Which is actually a good thing," he said, plopping himself down in Josh's favorite television chair, making himself at home.

Acting as if he owned the place.

As if Josh worked for him instead of the other way around.

"Why would that possibly be a good thing?" Molly said, not even wanting to be on the same planet with this guy, much less in the same room.

"Because I actually wanted to talk to you," he said. "A heart-to-heart."

Right away, Molly remembered one of the first things she'd heard that day at the hotel in New York and wanted to say to him, But you don't *have* a heart.

"No adults to bother us," he added, and Molly said, "Does that mean you don't count?"

Bobby Fishman said, "J.C. is always telling me what a clever kid you are."

She wished she were clever enough to come up with an excuse to go upstairs. Or just leave.

But she knew she was stuck until Mattie came back, that there were house rules, even though this wasn't her house—at least not yet—and that when she did get left alone she wasn't supposed to go anywhere. She knew that even as slowly as Mattie's pot roast was cooking in the kitchen—"Slower than I move," she'd said—that Mattie couldn't be gone *that* long. But Molly also knew that all the last-minute shoppers were probably out there now on the last Saturday before Christmas.

What a dope you are, she thought to herself, thinking nothing could possibly spoil tonight.

"The two of us have never really gotten a chance to talk," Bobby Fishman said.

He was wearing Nike sneakers that looked like the new pair Josh had been wearing. The green didn't really go with his jeans. He was wearing a sweater and a sports jacket and had his hair cut short, which only made Molly more aware of what a pointy head he had.

A pointy head and dark, buttonlike eyes.

She'd never understood what beady eyes really meant until now.

"I hear you talking to Josh all the time," Molly said, then couldn't keep herself from adding, "When you're on speaker phone, Mattie says everybody in the building can hear you."

He ignored that. Or maybe just didn't care. Maybe you couldn't hurt his feelings because he didn't have any, the way he didn't have a heart. Or maybe Bobby Fishman was like some kids she knew at school, the ones who weren't listening to you, they were just waiting for you to stop talking so they could start up again.

"So how's it going?" Bobby Fishman said. "With you and J.C., I mean."

Now Molly really couldn't help herself. "None of your business."

"See now, that's where you're wrong, kid," he said. "Anything that has to do with him is my business. Even when it's personal. That's just the deal."

"I'm not part of one of your deals."

He smiled. Only it didn't look like a real smile to Molly, it looked like some small dog baring its teeth.

"Funny you should mention deals," he said.

"No," Molly said. "You did."

Molly hoped against hope that Mattie or Josh would walk through the front door right now.

Only they didn't.

"You know anything about the sneaker deal I've been working on the past year?" he said.

"Not really."

"Want to?"

"Not really."

"Biggest shoe contract since LeBron," he said. "You know who he is, right?"

"I know a lot more than you think," Molly said. "And if you keep talking to me like I don't, I'm going upstairs to wait at Mattie's."

"Whoa," he said, putting out his hands. "Jump back, kid. Sometimes I forget I'm not talking to an owner." He waited for a response from Molly and when he didn't get one said, "That's a joke, kid. Most owners are a little slow out of the chutes."

Molly held her sides and put her head back as if she were laughing, except no sound came out.

"Okay, kid, I get it. You don't like me. I get a lot of that. So we can dispense with the small talk."

Molly waited.

"You want to know why this is going to be the biggest shoe deal in history? Because Josh Cameron isn't like the other guys."

"What other guys?"

"The bad guys."

"What bad guys?"

"The other stars of our NBA. Not all, mind you. But enough."

"L. J. Brown is a star, and he isn't a bad guy."

"Nope," Bobby Fishman said. "But he isn't in the upper echelon of stars, either. I'm talking about all those other guys with their attitudes." He bracketed *attitudes* with his fingers. "All those guys who tell you that they want you to love them and buy their stuff, but they don't want to be your role model, they'd rather act like a rock star or a rapper or some bling-bling thing."

"I have no idea what you're talking about," Molly said.

"I think you do. Because you're smart. Josh Cameron, from the day he got to the pros, has been marketed as the opposite of all that. The last boy next door. He doesn't get into trouble. He doesn't brag. He doesn't smoke or drink or cheat on his wife."

"He doesn't have a wife."

Molly looked at the front door again, begging it to open, wanting this to be over.

"I'm making a point, kid, about the world's greatest point guard."

"What does this have to do with me?" she said.

"Everything," Bobby Fishman said. "Josh Cameron can't have a daughter nobody ever knew about without having a wife nobody ever knew about to go with her."

In the distance, Molly heard church bells play "Silver Bells."

"Do I really have to draw you a picture?" Bobby Fishman said.

"People will understand," Molly said.

It was what she always told herself. Now she tried to tell Josh's terrier agent.

"No, they won't," he said.

Now all Molly could hear was the ticking of the grandfather clock from across the room.

"You know why his girlfriend hasn't been coming around? Because she knows about you. Because he told her he had to take pity on this kid belonging to an old girlfriend. Wait till she finds out you're his kid. You really think she's going to understand? And if *she* doesn't, how're his millions of fans going to understand?"

Before Molly could say anything, he kept going. "You will hurt him if you keep hanging around. Shake your head all you want, kid. Stick your fingers in your ears, for all I care. You're still hearing what I'm telling you. You will hurt him financially, and you will hurt his reputation. People will forgive him, sure, because people do in sports if you're a great enough player. They'll

212

forgive you for robbing a bank. But you *will* hurt him. He won't tell you that, so I'm telling you."

"You're wrong," Molly said. "You're twisting everything around."

"No," Bobby Fishman said, "I'm not. I'm actually trying to get everything straightened out here. It's time somebody at least told you the truth."

"Am I supposed to thank you now?" Molly said.

"You want to know what my full-time job really is these days? Keeping the media away from doing some heart-warming little feature on Josh and you. Telling them he's not doing this for publicity. You want to know the real reason? Because I'm not gonna let him look like a liar if the truth about you ever comes out."

He leaned forward so far that Molly was afraid he might pitch right over on the carpet.

This was what he must be like when he's closing one of his stupid deals.

"Oh, he'll try to do the right thing," Bobby Fishman said. "That's the kind of guy he is. But it will be the wrongest possible thing for Josh Cameron."

In a voice not much more than a whisper, he said, "Are you *that* selfish that you'd let him do something that will let people bring him down?"

Molly kept shaking her head. "It's not like that, what you're making it sound like."

Again in that soft voice he said, "You know it is. You're a smart kid, remember?"

He stood up.

"Do the right thing, kid. And get out of his life."

He walked over to the door, the one that never opened in time, and said, "I'm gonna leave now and let you think about what we've talked about."

"What *you* talked about," Molly said. She could feel angry tears pooling up in her eyes, she couldn't help it. She looked out the window again, trying to blink them away, not wanting to give him the satisfaction of seeing them.

"Somebody needed to tell you the truth. He knows this could never work, I know it could never work, now you need to know. It could never work. The press will have a field day with a guy they've treated like a hero his whole career. All because of you. It's why you gotta be the one who walks away from this. He never will. It's not his style."

Molly wanted to come up with the right words, find a better way to tell him how wrong he really was.

But she couldn't.

"You can blame this on me if you want," he said. "But the best thing for everybody, you and me particularly, is to act like this little chat of ours never happened. Keep this our little secret." He bracketed *secret* now and gave her one last scary smile. Even his teeth were small. "This is my job, kid," he said. "Making everybody see what's best for everybody concerned, even when they don't want to. Getting everybody on the same page."

Bobby Fishman, hand on the door handle, still not quite gone, said, "Don't get me wrong. He likes you, kid, he really does. But he doesn't want you around. Can't have you around, not for the long haul, anyway. He just hasn't figured out a way

to get rid of you without hurting you. But don't you hurt him because of that."

Then he left.

Molly did the same thing five minutes later, breaking the rule
about leaving, not caring about the house rules now. She left a
note in the kitchen saying she was going to have Thomas the
concierge walk her home and another note on the coffee table
next to the presents that said "Merry Christmas."

CHAPTER 26

*J*osh called the Evanses' house when he got back from Children's Hospital, wanting to know why Molly had left. Molly didn't come to the phone, just stayed in her bed and had Barbara say she'd eaten way too much junk at the game—too much junk always worked—and had gotten sick to her stomach.

Barbara wasn't buying that, Molly could tell, but did what Molly asked her anyway.

When she got off the phone, she came and stood in Molly's doorway.

"What happened?"

"Nothing happened."

"*Something* happened."

"No."

"I know you don't like opening up to me," she said. "Or anybody, with the possible exception of Sam Bloom. But could you make an exception just this once?"

"I'm fine," Molly said. "Other than my stomach, I mean."

"Sure you are," Barbara said. "I'm sorry I can't get a picture of your face right now. We could use it for Christmas cards next year. This is the way you looked when you got back from New York City."

Molly pulled the covers back up. "I was going to tell him we were moving," she said. "I guess it just put a big old knot in my stomach."

"I see," Barbara said, making a gesture with her hand that tried to take in Molly's whole room. "And speaking of moving, you haven't done much packing yet."

"Not much to pack."

Molly saw Kimmy scrunch into the doorway next to her mother. "I'll help, if you want," Kimmy said.

"Thanks," Molly said. "Maybe tomorrow. Right now I think the best thing would be to get some sleep."

Barbara hit the light switch next to the door, then came over and did something she hardly ever did, kissed Molly good night on the forehead.

"I'm sure he's in Los Angeles more than you think," she said. "Doesn't he have some kind of actress girlfriend out there?"

"Something like that."

"I know another move must seem hard," Barbara said. "But maybe a new city is the best way to start a new life. And like I said—"

"He's out there all the time," Molly said.

Barbara and Kimmy left. Molly lay there and stared up at the ceiling and tried to do what she used to do when she was little, tried to pretend that she was staring through the ceiling and the roof and all the way to the stars in the sky.

But she was tired of pretending.

Tired, period.

She wanted to hate Bobby Fishman more than she already did, make this all his fault.

But she knew what she really hated was him being right. It always stunk when grown-ups were right, about anything, especially a grown-up like him. All the pretending in the world couldn't make this work. She was going to leave him, go far away from him, the way her mom did. Maybe that's the way the story always had to end.

She had forgotten to turn her phone off. She heard it buzzing on her nightstand. Molly reached over and opened it up and saw Sam's name and phone number on her caller ID.

She hit the power button to turn it off and then tried her hardest to sleep until she finally did.

The next day, Sunday, was December 22.

Three days until Christmas.

Four until Los Angeles.

When she thought Josh would be awake, she screwed up her courage and called over there. Mattie answered.

Before Molly could ask if she could come over, Mattie said, "You all right? He said you were sick."

"My stomach's better," she said. "I'm fine now."

"Don't sound fine to me."

In a voice that sounded like she'd borrowed it from somebody else, some mean version of Molly Parker, Molly said, "I said I'm fine, Mattie."

There was a quiet at the other end of the phone that Molly could almost feel swallow her up, like she was Jonah getting swallowed up by the whale in the Bible story her mom used to read to her.

"Sorry," Mattie said finally.

"No," Molly said. "I'm sorry."

She tried to brighten up her voice. "So, can I come over? I've got some pretty cool news for you guys."

"Gimme about twenty minutes to wake the dead," she said.

Then Mattie said, "I'm waiting to open your present so I can give you yours at the same time."

Molly said "cool" again, not even asking if Josh had opened his yet.

"I waited as long as I could to tell you guys," Molly was saying in his living room. "But how cool is that, me getting a chance to go live in Hollywood?"

She had told them. Now she was telling them again, making this sound like the most exciting thing that had ever happened to anybody ever.

"LA," Josh said, like somehow he couldn't process the information Molly had just given them. "When?" he said.

Mattie didn't say anything.

"End of the week," Molly said.

"You're leaving . . . this week?" he said.

"Yup."

She looked over to the coffee table. There were two presents next to her presents, green wrapping paper instead of the red the Evanses used. It looked like a successful enough wrapping job on both of them that Mattie had to have done it.

"How long have you known?"

"I don't know. Not too long. Maybe a couple of weeks."

"You're moving to . . . LA?"

Molly tried her best to still be Miss Smart Mouth. "Is there an echo in here?" she said.

"How come you waited so long to tell us?" Josh said.

Mattie still wasn't saying anything.

"I guess I didn't want it to get in the way of anybody's Christmas, or whatever," she said. "But then I kind of figured I couldn't just leave, like, a note under the tree."

Their tree was upstairs, in Mattie's living room.

Now Mattie got up off the sofa and came across the room and put her arms around Molly.

"I can't say good-bye this close to saying hello, little girl," she said into Molly's hair.

Josh said, "You can't do this now."

"Guess our timing isn't so great, huh? Another one of those things that must run in the family." She swallowed hard and said, "But this is what I want. So be happy for me, okay?"

Josh nodded slowly, staring at the floor. He was sitting in his television chair, the one Bobby Fishman had sat in the day before. For a second, Molly thought about how happy Bobby Fishman was going to be when he heard the news. Molly thought, It'll feel like Christmas every day to him.

She clapped her hands, trying to look happy. "Let's open presents!" she said.

"Ho ho ho," Mattie said.

Mattie loved her beret, Molly could tell, but she wasn't any better at faking happiness than Molly was. She only liked the real thing. It was basically because Mattie was the happiest person Molly had ever known, at least this side of her mom.

Molly went next, opening Mattie's, yelling with delight— more fake happiness—when she saw Mattie had gotten her the new iPod nano that had been advertised all over the place during the Christmas season.

Molly knew the ad by heart.

"One thousand songs . . . ," she said.

"Impossibly small." Mattie finished the thought for her.

"I love it," Molly said.

"Glad I got it now," Mattie said. "Don't want you to be the one girl in Hollywood doesn't have one of these at the mall, or wherever they go out there."

Two presents left on the table.

Molly's and Josh's.

They agreed to unwrap at the same time.

Framed photographs.

Of Jen Parker.

They had each gotten each other the same thing.

It was like one of those times when you were with somebody and you both said the same thing at the exact same time. But the only thing Molly could say now, sounding like she was out of breath when she did, was, *"Whoa."*

He'd given her a picture her mom had given him when they were in college. Her mom in his leather jacket, that day he'd told her about, standing at the foot of the Rockefeller Plaza tree, the snow coming down.

She was laughing.

"Didn't know what to get you," he said. "Then I found this

the other day, at the bottom of this box of college stuff I kept meaning to toss out and never did. Now I'm glad I didn't. The only thing different is, I got a new frame."

Molly said, "It's perfect."

"Not the best photo quality in the world," he said. "I had to run that day we met at the tree and get a cheap camera, 'cause she insisted I take her picture. When we got it developed, she went and had it blown up to this size and gave it to me as a late Christmas present." He put his hands out. "It was better than anything I could think to buy you."

"I love it," Molly said.

"Not as much as I love this," he said.

The one Molly gave him was one of her and her mom skating. Molly was pretty sure it was the Greenwich rink in London, her mom wearing a red beret like the one Molly had gotten Mattie, trying to laugh it right off the top of her head. She and Molly had posed like ballerinas for the woman from the rink who they'd asked to take their picture, both of them up on their toes, arms up over their heads.

She had found it a couple of weeks ago, one of those nights going through her mom's letters and some other photographs. After she did, she took it over to FedEx Kinko's and had it blown up, then had it framed at this place Barbara liked on Charles Street.

Josh looked at it a long time and said, "That's her, all right."

If Molly didn't get out of here, she was going to start crying again. She felt like crying a lot these days. When she was with Mattie. When she was with Sam. Even with the hated Bobby Fishman.

She turned like she was looking at the big clock so she could close her eyes, hold the tears back one more time.

"Oh, man, look at the time," she said. "I've still got a *ton* of packing to do."

Josh said he had some time before practice, and then he had to meet with a few Nike guys who were in town, but that maybe they could grab some lunch right now.

"You know about this crazy sneaker deal, right?" he said.

Molly nodded, like, You bet. "Biggest in history," she said. "Bigger than LeBron's."

"So what about lunch?" he said. "You can pack later."

Molly said she'd love to, but she promised Sam she'd come over and help him with this big school project that was due to-morrow and he hadn't even started yet.

Lie. Whopper.

"But we're gonna see each other before you go, right?" he said. "Figure this out?"

"Absolutely!" Molly said.

Whopper number two.

She could feel Mattie's eyes on her now, like high beams from a car.

Mattie came over and hugged her again, as if she knew some-how that this was good-bye.

"Gonna miss you, Miss Miss," she said.

Molly said, "Barbara said I could come back a couple of times a year. And maybe you can come out when the Celtics play the Lakers. You'll probably get sick of me."

"Sure," Mattie said.

"Bobby says I spend any more time in LA than I do already, I should buy a place out there," Josh said.

Good old Bobby.

"And there's always summers, right?" Molly said.

"Right as rain," Mattie said.

Molly pulled back from her. "I really do gotta go," she said. "You know how impatient boys get."

They both offered to walk her down Beacon to Sam's. Molly waved them off. "Barbara gave me cab money because it's so cold out," Molly said. "So I'm good."

She put the picture of her mom back in its box.

I'm good?

That was a good one.

Ho ho ho.

CHAPTER 27

Molly thought she had already said the Big Good-bye to Josh. Barbara didn't know, apparently. Or didn't care. So without telling Molly, she had invited him over on Christmas Eve.

So now here he was, big as life, apologizing for showing up earlier than expected. He said he didn't have as much time as he thought he was going to have. Practice had been cancelled, and the team plane was leaving early for the Knicks game on Christmas. The big storm that had been forecast for today was supposed to hit Boston any time now, and the Celtics had to get the heck out of there before it did.

There were suitcases lined up near the bottom of the stairs in the front hall, like they were getting ready for some long family vacation. Mr. Evans was at the office, checking one last time to make sure he wasn't leaving anything important behind.

It was Josh, Molly and Barbara in the living room, big fire going.

The three of them and Kimmy.

Kimmy finally getting to meet her guy.

"I've heard a lot about you, Kimmy," he said, teasing with her a little bit.

Kimmy sort of knew he was but played along anyway, like she was playing her part, wheeling on Molly right away and saying, "What did you tell him about me?"

Molly didn't feel at all like playing along, but did, not wanting to ruin Kimmy's big moment, even though she just wanted this scene to be over.

"Just the basics," Molly said. "How your room is like a shrine to him, stuff like that."

"Liar!" Kimmy said. She was smiling, but her face had turned a color of red that reminded Molly of Gatorade fruit punch.

"I'm just kidding," Molly said. Molly the kidder. "I told him you were a big fan before I even knew who he was."

Kimmy said, "So would you sign some stuff for me?"

Everybody wants his name, Molly thought.

It was kind of funny, if you thought about it that way.

Kimmy ran upstairs, nearly tripping over one of the smaller suitcases, came back with a Sharpie, a Celtics cap, a color photograph of Josh, and a gray Celtics sweatshirt.

"Where'd you go?" Josh said. "The gift shop?"

Then he ran his hand through his hair. This is when he was at his best, when he was just going through the motions, when he could be the Josh everybody wanted.

Everybody except me, Molly thought.

He signed all the stuff, carefully writing out his name, and Kimmy watched every stroke as if the next one might do her in.

Barbara said, "We've already looked at the schedule. Bill—my husband—says the Celtics make their big West Coast trip in February."

"I think it starts Presidents' Day Weekend," Josh said.

"You'll be seeing Molly before you know it," she said.

"And me," Kimmy said.

"Right," Josh said, with a wink. "And you."

"We'll take good care of your friend here," Barbara said.

"Yeah," he said without too much enthusiasm.

"Well, I'll leave you guys alone." Barbara walked toward the door, realized Kimmy hadn't moved a muscle, was still standing there staring at Josh, all her freshly autographed stuff in her arms.

"Kimmy," her mom said. "I sort of meant that *we* would leave them alone."

Molly watched Kimmy back toward the door, wondering how much she knew, even though she'd never given Molly a hint that she knew anything more than that the two of them were friends because he'd been Molly's mom's boyfriend once.

The old cover story.

It seemed like such a big stinking deal once, keeping the secret. Now Molly almost didn't care. She felt like telling, as long as Kimmy would promise not to blab it all over e-mail the second she could get her computer fired up.

"Nice to meet you, Mr. Cameron," Kimmy said.

"Josh."

"Josh," she said.

Josh and Molly now.

There was soft Christmas music playing, a little bit louder than the sound of the fire. She could smell Barbara's pies baking.

"I'm no good at this," he said.

"Me neither."

"Listen," he said.

"I'm all ears."

"Now, there's a tone of voice I recognize."

She waited.

"All I'm trying to say is, we'll figure out a deal where we can see each other more than just West Coast trips," he said. "I mean, who says I can't fly you out once in a while, right?" He pointed at another pair of new sneakers. "It's not like I'm hurting for money, especially after the way Bobby killed Nike."

"Yeah," Molly said. "Killer deal."

"So we'll figure it out."

"You said that."

"We will."

"Got it."

Outside they both heard a car horn. He must have somebody driving him to the airport.

"Time to go," he said. "Sorry this had to be so rushed."

"What else is new?"

"I want to do the right thing, Molly," he said.

Bingo.

Saying it just like Bobby Fishman said he would.

"I know."

Nobody said anything. He leaned down, like he was going to give her a hug.

He'd never hugged her.

Not one single time.

She wasn't about to let him start today.

So Molly stepped back now, like she was doing her step-back imitation of him on the court, put her hand up instead and gave him a quick high-five.

"Good luck against the Knicks," she said.

"You gonna watch?"

"Wouldn't miss it."

Then he left. Molly listened to the new-sneaker squeak of his new-deal sneakers as he made his way to the front door.

Barbara had shipped some Christmas presents ahead to California. That way, she informed the rest of them, they could all have a second Christmas when they got to the house they'd be renting in a part of Los Angeles called Brentwood.

And, she said, calling herself Barb the Practical, they'd also have less stuff to take with them on the plane.

"We open the littler stuff here," she said. "Bigger stuff out there."

"I'll bet that's the way Mrs. Claus would have handled this kind of move for her and Santa," Molly said.

Christmas Eve dinner was with Mr. Evans's brother and his wife and their three teenage boys. Which meant, Molly knew from past, and extremely painful, experience, that as soon as dinner was over, it would be all video games all the time.

When they were finished with Barbara's Christmas pies—apple and pumpkin chiffon—Molly excused herself, saying she wanted to make sure she had her carry-on stuff all organized, and the stuff that was going into the big old leather suitcase that had belonged to her mom.

"Oh, you'll have time to do that tomorrow, won't you?"

Barbara said. "Why don't you go have some fun with the cousins?"

Yeah, Molly thought, that would be big fun on Christmas Eve, watching the Evans boys snort and squeal while they played *Madden '07* video football, or whatever year of snorting, squealing football they'd brought with them.

"Wait a second," Molly said, thinking faster than she had been lately. "You don't want me to be Molly the Practical?"

"Okay, girl, you got me there," Barbara said. "Go knock yourself out."

Molly went upstairs to her room and thought about calling Sam, then remembered he was at *his* cousins' place in Chestnut Hill for Christmas Eve dinner.

"Our annual musical," he'd said at school.

Molly asked what that meant, and Sam said, "Caroling."

He made it sound like the dirtiest word ever.

The way he said it made Molly laugh, even though she hadn't been doing much laughing lately, even with him.

"You have to sing?"

"We have to go from house to house and sing," he said. "Carrying our little songbooks."

Molly told him he looked more pathetic than Tiny Tim before things started to pick up for him in *A Christmas Carol.*

"You try hitting some of those 'First Noel' notes when you're freezing your buns off," he said.

Molly went now and sat in the window, watching the snow that had been forecast for Boston and the whole Northeast starting to come harder now, picturing Sam out there like some snowman built too wide at the bottom as he tried to keep his voice from cracking on the last couple of noels.

The snow was falling hard now.

For the last time in this house, she got out her mom's letters, the ones she'd taken from their box and placed in the folder she was going to put in her Celtics backpack—no way she was checking them through in her suitcase, suitcases could get lost—and read the last couple Jen had written.

The last one ended with this, not typed but written in her mom's handwriting: "Always believe you'll end up where you're supposed to be."

Right, she thought.

She snuck down the stairs to the front closet, hearing voices from the den, put on her parka and boots, and quietly went out the front door into the amazing night *whoosh* that snow made when it came down like this.

Molly walked toward Beacon Street, stopping sometimes to look behind her at the footprints she'd just made, watching how fast they were disappearing because the snow was really starting to accumulate now. When she got to the corner of Beacon and Joy—now there was a Christmas-sounding address if there ever was one—she stared across the park. Feeling the snow wet and cold on her face, she stared at the lights from the Ritz and from Two Commonwealth on the other side.

She closed her eyes, then opened them.

Maybe there'd be some kind of sign over there, the kind of sign that her mom used to say was all around you, if you knew how to look.

A sign telling her to go or stay.

There wasn't a single light on either of his two floors.

Molly knew Mattie had gone to North Carolina to visit family down there. He was long gone on the team plane.

Nobody home.

She turned and headed back.

olly wasn't particularly big on clothes, never had been, though she knew she looked decent in pretty much whatever she wore. People were always telling her how nice she looked, that she could look dressed up when she wasn't even trying.

But even she knew that the three pairs of Seven jeans that Barbara got for her, the first present she opened on Christmas morning, were a big deal.

Mr. Evans got her a portable DVD player.

"Perfect for long flights, kiddo," he said.

Kimmy gave her Oakley sunglasses.

"I don't even own a pair of sunglasses," Molly said, giving Kimmy a hug.

"I know," Kimmy said. "That's why I got these for you. It would be like going to Los Angeles without wearing pants."

When they had finished opening their presents—Molly had gotten them short-sleeved Lacoste polo shirts the day she'd shopped at Louis—they sat down for what Barbara described as their traditional Christmas breakfast.

Blueberry muffins, fresh grapefruit.

And bratwurst.

"It just sort of evolved over time," Barbara explained to Molly.

When they had all cleaned up, Mr. Evans and Barbara said they were off to another Christmas tradition of theirs, serving food to the homeless at a soup kitchen over near the Garden. They said that last year they'd taken Kimmy with them, but now that the storm had turned into a full nor'easter, the girls could stay home.

Before they left, Molly asked if Sam could come over, as long as it was all right with Kimmy.

"It's Christmas," Kimmy said. "I promise to be nice."

Barbara said they'd be back sometime in the afternoon and that if anybody got hungry—"She means Sam, obviously," Kimmy said—there was plenty of leftover roast beef from last night. Mr. Evans told Molly they could watch the Celtics game later.

"Cool," she said.

When Mr. Evans and Barbara were gone, bundled for the outside as if they were going to the North Pole, Kimmy went to her room to try on her own new jeans and a new summery dress her mom had gotten for her. Molly went to her room, back to the window, watching the snow a little more, like she was saving up in her mind how it looked, knowing that tomorrow she was moving to a place where it was never going to snow, where Sam said her whole world was going to be the same weather report every day.

"Warm and sunny," he'd said. "Makes me feel all warm and fuzzy."

She had wondered all along how she would feel when it was

time to leave. It turned out today was the same as all the other days lately, even though it was Christmas Day.

She was just plain old sad.

Mostly because she had been so sure, for a while anyway, that things might actually work out the way they were supposed to.

Silly girl.

She turned away from the window. There on the corner of her desk, the last thing on it, was the picture of her mom Josh had given her. Molly felt as if her mom were looking right at her.

"Tell me what to do," Molly said, not even caring what Kimmy would think if she walked in and saw Molly talking to herself.

"How come when I need you the most to tell me what to do," she said, "you're not here?"

She hopped off the high windowsill, and as she did, she landed funny, like a bad landing in skating. She banged against the desk and hit it pretty hard, knocking the photograph of her mom to the floor.

For a moment, Molly's heart sank. She thought she'd broken it.

But when she knelt to pick it up, she saw that only the back had come off, the part with the leg attached to it that made the frame stand up.

That's when she saw her mom's handwriting on the back of the photograph.

"Always believe you'll end up where you're supposed to," it said.

Same as in her letter.

Word for word.

Molly stared at the writing, turned the picture back around so she could look at her mom, wearing his jacket, standing in front of the tree.

Believe.

She heard the doorbell then.

Sam.

Molly, her heart pounding so hard against her chest it was like it was trying to crash right out of her, ran down the front steps at full speed, taking them two or three at a time.

Only she wasn't running away from anything this time.

She was completely out of breath when she opened the door to the snow, and Sam Bloom.

"Whoa, girl," he said. "Where you going?"

"New York," Molly said.

CHAPTER 29

*Y*ou're going to New York, in a blizzard, on Christmas Day, to see a basketball game?" Sam said.

"Pretty much."

"Do I get to ask why?"

"It's a long story," Molly said. "And I don't have a lot of time."

"How do you plan to go, by sleigh?"

"Nah," Molly said. "Even Santa would be grounded today."

"So how? Dog sled?"

"I'm thinking train."

Sam had walked over. He took off his cap, shook the snow off it.

"Even Rudolph's nose wasn't as red as yours," Molly said. "Now, c'mon, we gotta see when the next train leaves for New York. Barbara and Mr. Evans are gone until the afternoon. I've gotta be on my way by then."

"We," Sam Bloom said.

"What?"

"I said *we* have to be on our way to New York."

He crossed his arms across the front of his thick parka, as if to say that's it and that's all.

"Your mom will never let you do this," Molly said.

"Who said anything about telling my mom?"

They were in Molly's room, door shut, on her laptop, looking at the Amtrak schedules.

"Aha!" Sam said.

"Aha?"

"It's what they say in the old movies when they've discovered a clue," he said.

"Oh."

"The next train, and it's their fastest, is an Acela Express," he said. "Number two-two-five-three. Leaves here at eleven-fifteen, arrives in the Big Apple at two-forty-two in the afternoon."

Molly said, "That's in, like, forty-five minutes. Forget it, we can never get over to South Station by then."

"South Station?" Sam said. "What kind of a travel agent do you think you're working with here?"

"Where then?"

"Back Bay, right across from Nieman-Marcus."

"We can walk there!" Molly said.

"My point exactly," Sam said. "Just another walk in the winter wonderland. Can't wait. I feel like I should be pulling a dog sled."

"Woof," Molly said. "Woof."

Then she looked at him. "You don't have to do this."

"Nobody said I did," Sam said. "But here's another thing from the old movies: The hero needs a trusty sidekick. And I'm yours."

"Yeah," Molly said. "You are."

Sam said, "You think it's too late to make a reservation?"

Molly, looking over his shoulder, suddenly felt herself sag. She went over and sat down on her bed.

"What's the point?" she said. "We can't go."

Sam said, "I know women change their minds, but this has to be some kind of record."

"Tickets cost ninety-five dollars," Molly said, pointing at the screen. "We don't have enough money. And I don't have a credit card. Do you?"

"My mom says we can talk about it when I'm thirty."

"So there's no way," Molly said.

She sat and pictured a scoreboard showing time running out. Sam came over and plopped down next to her.

"Man," he said. "Where's mad money when we really need it?"

Molly turned, eyes wide, and slapped him on the arm.

"Ow?" he said.

"You're a genius!" Molly said.

"I'm aware of that," he said. "But why this time?"

"I never gave you your mad money back from the last time I went to New York, that's why!"

She jumped off the bed, ran over to her backpack, unzipped a side pocket, and pulled out the envelope with Sam's stash in it.

"Aha!" she said.

Now Sam was the one who looked sad.

"Not exactly," he said.

"Explain."

"You spend any money in New York?"

"A few dollars when I ran off that day, that was it."

"I gave you everything I had," Sam said. "One hundred and twenty dollars. That means the price of one ticket, with a little left over."

"Only one of us can go," Molly said.

"No," Kimmy said from across the room. "You can both go."

Molly hadn't even heard the door open.

"I'll loan you guys the money," Kimmy said, standing there in the doorway.

"You heard?" Molly said.

"Not all of it," she said. "I did have to try some clothes on. But I heard enough."

She smiled. "Don't you know that I hear everything around here?"

She told them to hold on, ran out of the room in her new Seven jeans, and was back in about a minute, a neat stack of money in her hand.

"There's enough," she said. "I counted it."

The best Molly could do was "thank you."

"I'll cover for you guys with my parents," Kimmy said. "Now go see your dad."

"You know?" Molly said.

Kimmy gave her a look like she was the slowest kid at the Prescott School for Good Girls and Boys.

"What part of 'I hear everything' aren't you hearing?" Kimmy said. "Now, go or you'll miss your train."

The fast train went slow, because of the snow on the tracks, the conductor kept saying. So it was nearly four-thirty when they finally heard the announcement that they were a few minutes from "Penn Station, Eighth Avenue and Thirty-Fourth Street, New York City."

"Hey," Sam said. "Isn't that your favorite movie? *Miracle on 34th Street*?"

"It is," Molly said.

"So this can be like your version of it," Sam said.

"The miracle is that we're here," Molly said. "But we've still got a few more miracles to go."

They had decided that Sam wouldn't call his mom until they got to New York, since neither one of them knew if there was some way Amtrak could stop the train if they thought they had runaway kids on board. The story they'd cooked up: He'd tell her that Molly was going, and he couldn't let her go alone, but that it was all right, Josh was meeting them at the train.

Sam said, "So we're basically telling only one little white lie for a white Christmas?"

"The part about Josh."

Sam said, "I can work this gig."

He walked down to the end of the car and Molly could hear him talking fast.

At the very end, Molly didn't hear the white lie. Just the classic cell-phone lie of all time.

"Mom? We're breaking up . . . can you hear me? I love you, too . . . I'll call you after the game. . . ."

He came back, pumping his fist, and sat back down next to Molly.

"When you're good, you're good," he said.

"Except," Molly said, "when you're great."

The train pulled in. They followed the rest of the passengers up a long stairway and into what looked like the main station, about ten times bigger than Back Bay station, more crowded than Molly thought it could ever be on Christmas Day afternoon, with people arriving in New York or getting ready to leave New York, the huge board with the announcements and track numbers constantly changing.

"How do we know where to go at the Garden to have them find Josh?" Sam said.

"It doesn't matter," Molly said. "We're not going there."

They got out of the cab and ran past Radio City Music Hall, past the sign across the street that said "NBC Studios."

They came around the corner, Sam grumpy and wet and saying "mush," and came to a dead stop because there it was:

The biggest Christmas tree in the world, lights on. The lights looked even brighter because of the snow and because it was almost dark now. Molly put her head back as far as it would go and felt like she was looking up at the tallest skyscraper in New York. Or anywhere.

There were more people than Molly expected, even in this snow. Just as Molly and Sam got there, one couple handed their disposable camera—like the one Josh said he'd used that time—to the security guard, asking him to take a picture of them, moving the guard back so he could get as much of the tree as possible into the shot.

Sam wasn't looking at the couple.

He was looking up at the tree.

"Wow," he said.

"You can say that again."

"Wow."

"It was a figure of speech," Molly said.

"Sorry if I don't know all my lines," he said.

Molly took him by the arm.

"C'mon," she said.

Sam said, "Where are we going now?"

"Skating," Molly said.

She had told him the story about her mom and Josh and the Holiday Festival and the tree in the cab.

"I need to be skating when he gets here," she said.

Sam said, "Where are we?"

"New York."

"Very funny," he said. "I mean the exact address."

"Forty-ninth Street, I'm pretty sure."

"Miracle on Forty-ninth," he said. "That's what we're looking for here."

Molly said that worked for her.

When they got to the bottom of the steps, Sam said, "Mols, what if he doesn't come? He thinks you're in Boston. He's getting ready to play a game on national TV."

"He'll be here," Molly said.

That's when she saw the sign. "Rockefeller Plaza Skating CLOSED Christmas Day."

CHAPTER 30

*I*t was five-thirty now.

The game was scheduled for seven.

"It was supposed to be open," she said.

"But it's not, Mols."

"I was supposed to skate, and he was supposed to be up there," she said.

"You're not going to cry, are you?" he said. "Please don't. I hate it when you cry."

"I'm not crying," she said. "I'm mad."

"Okay," he said. "You're mad. I'm cold."

"He'll still be here," Molly said.

Sam didn't say anything, just started up the stairs, so Molly followed him. They walked back to the base of the tree, where Molly had seen the star that time.

Sam pointed through the opening on the street to their right.

"Hey, see that diner?" he said. "I think it's open."

"You can't be hungry. You ate three times on the train," she said. "I was afraid you were going to clean out the rest of our money."

"No, I'm *not* hungry," he said, "but I need some hot chocolate bad."

"Fine," she said.

"You'll wait here?"

"I'm not going anywhere," Molly said. "Get me one, too."

He put the back of his glove across his face to get the snow off it.

"We can't stay forever, Mols," he said. " 'Cause then this will get real crazy. Not that it isn't already."

"See if they can put whipped cream on mine," she said.

Sam the Snowman, trusty sidekick, trudged slowly through the snow. Molly went back to the railing and looked down at the rink, where the movie was supposed to end. The ice was covered evenly by the snow, like the thick, white comforter she had on her bed.

Sam was right.

It had been crazy all along.

She started to cry then. No need to fight back her tears anymore, no need to hide them. Nobody there to see. Molly cried hard, the tears blurring her eyes as much as the snow did.

"You were supposed to be down there," a voice from behind her said.

She turned around.

And there he was.

No cap today, hiding his face from the fans. So it looked like his hair had turned white.

He was wearing the leather jacket.

Molly said, "The stupid rink was closed."

"So, anyway," he said, like they were already halfway into the conversation, "I'm waiting to get on the bus with the rest of the guys, and I'm thinking this is gonna be my one shot to see the tree this year. So I told Coach I was gonna walk to the Garden."

"Even in the snow?" Molly said.

"Snow never bothered me before when I had to get to this tree," he said. "Plus, sometimes you meet the best people here you'll ever meet in your life."

Molly, being Molly, forever Molly, put her hands on her hips then, cocked her head.

"Hey," she said, "don't you have a game to play?"

He scooped her up into his arms, lifting her like she didn't weigh anything at all, like she was as light as the snow, as if he wanted to lift her all the way to the top of the tree and sit her on top of it.

Then he was hugging Molly finally, and she was hugging him back.

"First I had to come get my daughter," he said.